The committee members filed back into the room. They seemed to move in slow motion, every minute dragging. Would they find James guilty of sexual assault—or was Jessica really the one on trial?

"Ms. Wakefield, with regard to your charge, this committee finds that you have not sufficiently proven your case." Dean Shreeve sat back and looked directly into Jessica's eyes.

Jessica felt herself being hurled back to reality with tremendous force. *It was all a waste of time*, she realized. She should never have come forward.

"Furthermore, I suggest that you seek counseling," the dean continued. "False accusations are very destructive, Ms. Wakefield. They ruin people's lives." His voice was full of contempt.

"Take me home," Jessica cried to Elizabeth. "I can't take it anymore. Please, just take me home."

Bantam Books in the Sweet Valley University series
Ask your bookseller for the books you have missed

And don't miss these
Sweet Valley University Thriller Editions:

SWEET VALLEY UNIVERSITY®

Take Back the Night

Written by
Laurie John

Created by
FRANCINE PASCAL

BANTAM BOOKS
NEW YORK · TORONTO · LONDON · SYDNEY · AUCKLAND

RL 6, age 12 and up

TAKE BACK THE NIGHT
A Bantam Book / April 1995

Sweet Valley High® *and Sweet Valley University*™
are trademarks of Francine Pascal
Conceived by Francine Pascal
Produced by Daniel Weiss Associates, Inc.
33 West 17th Street
New York, NY 10011

ISBN: 0-553-56656-3

Published simultaneously in the United States and Canada

Bantam Books are published by Bantam Books, a division of Bantam
Doubleday Dell Publishing Group, Inc. Its trademark, consisting of the
words "Bantam Books" and the portrayal of a rooster, is Registered in
U.S. Patent and Trademark Office and in other countries. Marca
Registrada. Bantam Books, 1540 Broadway, New York, New York 10036.

PRINTED IN THE UNITED STATES OF AMERICA

OPM   0 9 8 7 6 5 4

To Megan Walsh

Chapter One

"Let go of me!" Jessica Wakefield screamed. The sound of her voice echoed through the empty parking lot. "James! Stop it!"

No one was around. James Montgomery grabbed Jessica and dragged her to a dark, wooded area on the edge of Lookout Point. He pushed her to the ground with the same force he used on the football field, knocking the wind out of her. He pinned her arms to her sides and tried to kiss her. Jessica turned her head away.

"What's the matter with you?" James slurred, burying his face in her neck. "I take you out for a romantic dinner and this is the thanks I get?"

Jessica coughed. The smell of alcohol on his breath was overpowering. "Stop it, James! I'm not joking. Get off me!" She gasped for air—the weight of his body was crushing her. Jessica ignored the wave of nausea that hit her, fighting to stay conscious.

James's face was a blur. She felt his hands moving

1

all over her body, trying to unhook her bustier top, tugging at her pants. He moved off her for a moment as he started to undo his belt. Fresh air filled Jessica's lungs, clearing her head and giving her strength. Jessica pushed his shoulders back, struggling to get away from him. For one brief second he seemed to lose his balance, but he quickly regained it and came back at her with a painful jab to the ribs.

"Stop playing games!" James yelled at her angrily. He looked around. "Get back in the car!"

Everything would be all right, Jessica told herself over and over again as he dragged her toward the red Miata. Any second now, Elizabeth would be there. Her sister would take her away from this.

James threw her forcefully onto the front seat, smacking Jessica's head against the steering wheel. Her head started to throb in time with the hot pain in her ribs. Jessica listened for the roar of Elizabeth's Jeep pulling into the parking lot. She waited to hear the sound of shattering glass as her sister smashed the Miata's windshield. But it was completely quiet. The only sound Jessica heard was James breathing heavily in her ear.

"Where are you, Elizabeth?" Jessica shouted desperately. "Where are you?"

"I'm right here, Jess," a voice answered.

Jessica slowly opened her eyes. Hazy images passed in front of her, moving in time with the pounding in her head. Shapes and colors swirled around her. Jessica shrank back in fright, covering her face with her hands.

2

"It's all right," the voice said gently. "You're safe now."

Jessica rubbed her eyes. Her identical twin sister, Elizabeth, hovered over Jessica's bed. It was morning. She wasn't at Lookout Point, but in the safety of her room in Dickenson Hall.

Jessica took a deep breath to calm her racing heart. She closed her eyes. An image of James materialized, his strong hands ready to strike her at any moment. She quickly sat up in bed, keeping the covers pulled carefully over her shoulders.

A look of concern clouded Elizabeth's blue-green eyes. "What is it?" she asked, reaching for her sister's hand. "Are you OK?"

Jessica turned her body, and a sharp pain shot through her rib cage. She delicately touched the back of her head. There was an egg-shaped bump near the base of her skull. The dull ache of her head made her feel woozy. A tear rolled down Jessica's cheek as she remembered that her terrible date with James hadn't been just a nightmare. It had been brutal reality.

"Try to rest, Jess," Elizabeth said soothingly. Jessica tried to relax as she watched her twin open their small refrigerator. Elizabeth looked almost motherly in her bathrobe and slippers, her long blond hair wrapped tightly in a bun. She filled a plastic bag with ice and wrapped it in a towel.

"It really happened, didn't it?" Jessica asked somberly. She lifted the top of her purple satin pajamas and placed the ice gently on her ribs. Overnight the

3

bruise had swelled and turned a dark blue. There were four small round bruises on her arm where James had grabbed her. They looked like fingerprints. "It wasn't just a bad dream."

Elizabeth moved the ice pack and looked at the bruise. "Maybe we should take you to the infirmary. This doesn't look so good."

"I'll be fine," Jessica answered, hastily replacing the ice pack. She sat up quickly to prove her point, gritting her teeth to hide the pain.

Elizabeth touched Jessica's forehead. "Jess, you really should see a doctor," she persisted.

Jessica frowned. Just because Elizabeth had been born four minutes earlier, she thought it automatically entitled her to boss Jessica around. Jessica came to college to be independent. To make her own decisions, even if she didn't always make the right ones. *I'm not a child anymore—I'm a grown woman,* Jessica thought resolutely. If she didn't want to see the doctor, there was nothing Elizabeth could do about it. She turned to her sister. "I'm not going, and that's it."

Elizabeth put the cold pack behind Jessica's head. "I don't understand you—don't you want to feel better?"

"It's not that," she said as the coolness eased the throbbing in her head. "Once doctors start looking at me, they're going to want to know how this happened. And a game of twenty questions is the last thing I'm in the mood for."

4

Elizabeth stared at her. "You don't want anyone to know about what James did to you?"

"No, not really." Jessica paused. "Well, maybe. I don't know what I want. Right now, I'd rather not think about it." Jessica's vision blurred as a fresh batch of tears welled up in her eyes. "I don't remember if I thanked you last night, but I'm really grateful that you came to my rescue. Thanks for being there, Liz." She gave her sister a hug.

Elizabeth smiled weakly. "Anytime, sis," she said softly.

Jessica's throat tightened. With some effort, she climbed out of bed before the tears started to roll down her cheeks. "I think I'm going to take another shower," she said hoarsely.

"Be careful of your ribs. They're still swollen," Elizabeth said. She handed Jessica a clean towel. "Are you sure you're OK? Do you need anything?"

"I'm fine," Jessica answered. The terry-cloth robe she wrapped around herself was familiar and comforting. Jessica grabbed her soap dish and some shampoo and opened the door. Lying in the hallway, right in front of their door, was a pink carnation with a note attached. Jessica picked it up.

"Who is that from?" Elizabeth asked.

Jessica shrugged. She read the note aloud. "It says 'Jessica, I hope you feel better soon.'"

"You don't think it's from the same person who left your purse at the door last night, do you?"

Jessica wondered. The flower must have been left

by someone who knew about what happened at Lookout Point. Probably the same someone who had followed them last night and who picked up the purse Jessica had left behind at the Mountain Lodge Inn. Whoever this person was, they seemed to be looking after her. Jessica held the carnation to her nose, breathing in its sweet scent. Who could it be?

It wasn't until Jessica slipped out into the hallway that Elizabeth let the tears flow. Stress and anger had been building up inside her since last night, and now she couldn't hold it in anymore. Elizabeth threw herself onto her bed and cried in her pillow.

Why did this have to happen to Jessica? she wondered sadly. It was so unfair. Jessica had had more than her share of trouble since the twins started college. First she'd fallen in love with Michael McAllery and practically dropped out of school to be with him. They'd eloped and Jessica had kept their marriage a secret from nearly everyone, including their parents. Their marriage had been rough. Jessica eventually realized she had made a mistake and tried to leave Mike, but he'd been drunk and come after Jessica with a gun. When their brother, Steven, tried to protect her, the gun accidentally went off and Mike was shot. He was paralyzed.

Their marriage ended in an annulment. Mike went through therapy and was recovering. Jessica returned to school, hoping to resume a normal life. After several confrontations with the snobby Theta vice-president, Jessica had rejoined her sorority and started building relationships with her Theta sisters. Now, just as things were settling down and Jessica's life was getting back to normal, James Montgomery had to enter her life.

Elizabeth dried her eyes and breathed deeply. She raised the window blinds, letting the first few rays of early-morning sunlight warm her swollen face. Her heart was heavy. Jessica's problems weren't entirely because of bad luck—she was also partly to blame. If there was one thing Jessica was often guilty of, it was letting her emotions guide her decisions. Elizabeth was always the more rational, responsible of the two, and she was usually an excellent judge of character. But somehow James slipped by her.

James had seemed charming and polite whenever Elizabeth had spoken with him. He was handsome, a good student, and a football star. He had a great reputation around campus. There was no reason to think he wasn't a good date for her sister. Still, a pang of guilt gnawed at her. If only she had picked up on James's violent tendencies. Maybe she could have stopped Jessica from going out with him.

Elizabeth reached down and picked up Jessica's discarded clothes from the floor. *Even if I had stopped Jessica from going out with him, he probably would have done the same thing to someone else*, Elizabeth reasoned. It wouldn't have been difficult. There were tons of girls on campus who would jump at the chance to go out on a date with James Montgomery.

Maia Stillwater had. Maia was in Elizabeth's journalism class, and they'd worked on a sexual-politics project together. At the time, Elizabeth had noticed that whenever they talked about gender issues, Maia tensed up. After a lot of coaxing Maia finally confessed that she'd gone out with a guy a few weeks before and that he had raped her. But she'd refused to tell Elizabeth who the guy was.

It wasn't until last night, when Maia stopped by after Jessica had gone out on her date, that Elizabeth found out the truth. James had taken Maia to the Mountain Lodge Inn for dinner, and then to Lookout Point. That was where he'd raped her.

A chill ran through Elizabeth as she pulled her robe tightly around her. Elizabeth had managed to get to her sister before James had a chance to rape her. But someone else might not be so lucky. First Maia, now Jessica. Elizabeth shuddered. Who would be next?

Over half an hour had passed when Jessica came back in, drying her hair with a towel. "I'm finally starting to feel human again."

Elizabeth gave her a thin smile. "I'm glad you're feeling better. I just want you to know, if you want to talk about last night—"

"I really don't," Jessica cut in. "I just don't want to think about it right now."

Elizabeth nodded as she poured steaming coffee into two mugs. She didn't want to push her sister if she wasn't ready to talk about it. At the same time,

Elizabeth couldn't ignore the feeling of urgency rising within her. While Jessica was making up her mind about how to deal with the situation, James was free, roaming the campus. *We've got to stop him,* Elizabeth thought anxiously. *Before it's too late.*

"I knew you'd come back for me, Tisiano!" Lila Fowler shouted with relief. *"I knew you wouldn't leave me here to die."*

Tisiano walked silently through the debris from the plane crash to where Lila was trapped by the Cessna's twisted frame. Lila melted at the sight of her husband's thick dark hair and eyes as green and warm as the Mediterranean Sea. She was afraid to touch him at first, imagining that he was just a ghost and her hand would pass right through him. When Tisiano reached for her, Lila was filled with joy as she felt his strong, solid body next to her. In his arms, she was safe.

"I'll always be here for you, Lila," he whispered softly in her ear, lifting her from the wreck.

Lila wrapped her arms tightly around his neck. "Please don't ever leave me again," she sobbed passionately. *"I've been so lonely without you."*

Tisiano kissed her tenderly. "Just remember, mi amore, *no matter what happens, I'll always be here for you."*

Lila felt a shiver run the length of her body. They were finally together again, just as she had dreamed about. As soon as they left the mountain, they would be ready to start their new lives together. They would never be apart again. Lila clung to Tisiano, squeezing him tighter and tighter and tighter . . .

Lila woke with a start. An icy blast of mountain air ripped through the Sierra Nevada, chilling any warmth she might have felt from the rays of the morning sun. A tiny squirrel dove into the hollow of a tree, trying to find shelter from the wind.

She looked up at the wreckage scattered around her. It had been several months since Tisiano had died in a Jet-Ski accident, yet she still dreamed about him almost every night. Even after the plane crash, Tisiano's face was the only thing she saw when she closed her eyes. It was nice to be reunited with him in her dreams, but Lila bitterly resented having to come back to reality.

I don't know what's worse, Lila thought grimly, *waking up to find that Tisiano's still dead, or waking up to find that I still haven't been rescued.*

Lila glanced at the body beside her and scowled. *Or maybe the worst thing of all is waking up to find myself locked in an embrace with Bruce Patman.* Even though it felt like they were in the middle of a blizzard, Bruce was sleeping soundly, a tranquil smile on his face. The thin wool blanket they were supposed to share was wrapped snugly around him.

That's just like him, Lila thought with irritation as she tugged at one corner of the blanket, reclaiming her half. If she had to be stranded on an isolated mountaintop with someone, why did it have to be Bruce I-Love-Myself-More-Than-Anything Patman? Trying

10

not to freeze or starve to death was hard enough without also having Bruce's ego to contend with.

Lila pressed her body against Bruce's to stay warm. Of course, even being stuck with Bruce was better than being in the wilderness all alone. And as much as she hated to admit it, the arrogant jerk did occasionally have his good moments. In fact, the day before he had even made a valiant attempt at fishing so they wouldn't starve to death. Unfortunately the only thing he'd caught was a fever.

She had spent most of the night looking after him. Lila trembled when she remembered his pasty, sweaty face and burning forehead. The sight of Bruce shaking and talking deliriously had been chilling. Worst of all was that helpless feeling in the pit of her stomach. She'd had no idea how to help him. If Bruce had died, it would have been her fault.

Lila sighed with relief as she touched Bruce's cool forehead. His fever had broken. Soon he'd be well enough to make fun of her like he always did.

Lila impulsively checked his forehead again. His skin was more than just cool, it was *cold*. Lila shivered and recoiled instantly, as if she had just received an electric shock. Studying his face, Lila noticed that his skin was still pale and his lips were purplish around the edges. Her heart stopped. Carefully she bent over his motionless figure. She listened closely for the sound of his breathing.

Bruce was very quiet, and his chest was still. Lila began to panic. *What do I do?* Her mind raced. She

11

gently nudged his shoulder. "Come on, Bruce. Wake up," she said. His hand, which had been resting on his stomach, limply fell to his side. Lila covered her mouth to keep from screaming.

Please let Bruce be OK, she begged silently. She thought of all the times she had been mean to him, how she had relished giving him a hard time. If Bruce lived through this, she vowed never to harass him again.

"Wake up!" she shouted, louder this time. She shook him by the shoulders and slapped his face. After losing Tisiano, Lila was terrified of being left alone again. Another gust of cold air blew through the mountain valley, chilling Lila to the bone. "Wake up!" she cried hysterically.

William White scanned the library stacks to see if anyone was around. Hearing footsteps in the hallway, William strategically placed his wheelchair between two rows of study carrels in the dark microfiche room. Judging from the sound, he could tell that the footsteps belonged to Maeve, the reference librarian who had a passion for platform shoes.

William had spent enough time in the library to know everyone's daily routines and even details about their personal lives. For example, he knew that Maeve came here once a day to drop off the new microfiche. But William also knew that Maeve collected ceramic unicorns, never went out on Friday nights, and avoided shellfish because it made her deathly ill.

William was proud of all the useful bits of information he'd managed to collect over the last few weeks. Thanks to Elizabeth Wakefield, he was becoming a master at surveillance.

Hurry up, Maeve, William thought impatiently, *or I'll sneak some lobster in your sandwich at lunch.* Even though it was handy to know so much about people, it was a shame that he found them all to be so dull and stupid. Especially the security guards at the Harrington Mental Institution, where William tried to spend as little time as possible. So far, slipping out whenever he pleased was incredibly easy. Even if, by some outside chance, they managed to catch him, William was certain he could talk himself out of any situation. He could make anyone believe anything.

Maeve closed a file drawer and left the room. When it was clear, he jumped out of the wheelchair and stretched his legs, which were sore from having to stay completely still for hours at a time. His fake beard was itchy, and his brown wig was stifling. At times, he wondered if it was all worth it. Then he would picture Elizabeth's beautiful face and know that it was. She wasn't like anyone else he had ever met. Elizabeth was extremely intelligent. She appreciated the finer things in life, like literature and classical music. They were a perfect match.

He folded the wheelchair, then unlocked the door to the neglected storage closet. The closet was hardly bigger than the tiny room he had at the institution, but it was much more comfortable. He had furnished it with items he found scattered in various parts of the library. In one corner there was a small table, a reading lamp, and a folding chair. He'd found an old cot in the basement that the janitor used to take naps during his lunch hour and a brand-new coffeemaker in the lounge. He'd emptied the shelves of ancient cleaning supplies, then filled them again with volumes of poetry that he took from the stacks.

William switched on the light. Dozens of photographs of Elizabeth smiled at him. William sighed contentedly. His favorite picture had been taken the night of the charity ball, when they had still been a couple. It was the last night he remembered being truly happy. Elizabeth had been absolutely gorgeous in her black evening gown. He loved the way she gazed deeply into his eyes while they were dancing, the way she moved under his touch . . .

He hadn't thought there was any harm in bringing her back to his apartment to drink some wine. But it was there that she snooped around and looked through his books when he wasn't watching. That was how she discovered his link to the powerful secret society. William, Peter Wilbourne, and Celine Boudreaux had plotted to stop Elizabeth from leaking the information to the press, but Boy Wonder Tom Watts had come to her rescue. If only Elizabeth had kept her nose out of his business, she would have never known a thing. And if she hadn't help put him away, then William wouldn't have to go to such lengths to be near her. If things had gone differently, he would still be the love of her life instead of that idiot Tom Watts. William laughed bitterly. *Enjoy her while you still can, Tommy boy,* he thought. *She'll be mine soon.*

There was a soft knock at the door. It slowly opened.

"Celine!" William exclaimed sharply. "What took you so long?"

Celine Boudreaux's honey-blond curls were tousled and her form-fitting minidress was wrinkled. She looked agitated. "What took so long?" she mimicked, her southern drawl reaching a fever pitch. "I'll tell you what! I've been trapped in this stupid library for almost two hours, trying to find my way around. I got lost in the dictionary aisle."

"This isn't a supermarket, Celine. It's called the reference section," William corrected smugly. He laughed as he thought about clueless Celine, wandering through the library, not knowing the archives from the periodicals.

"Whatever," Celine snapped. She lit a cigarette and kicked off her high heels. "Why do we have to meet in here, anyway? Why can't we meet at my place?"

"Because we can't be seen together, that's why," William answered. "Just be glad I found this abandoned room, where we can be relatively free in our actions." William enjoyed manipulating Celine's infantile emotions. All it took was the right word or look, and he could have her as loose and playful as a new puppy. He was in complete control.

"Come here," he said silkily, motioning for her to sit on his lap. "I'm sorry you had so much trouble, but I'm glad you're here. I need you." He kissed her aggressively.

Celine giggled. She coyly twirled a blond curl around her finger and smiled. "Hey, sugar, how about you and me sneak back to my place tonight? We could have a little sleepover party."

William took a drag from her cigarette. "I can't, Celine," he said coldly as he exhaled. "I have to get back to the hospital tonight before lights out. Andrea's been out sick."

"Is she the little wench who's been covering for you at bedtime?"

William nodded almost imperceptibly.

"Just what have you been doing for her in return?" Celine pouted.

"Now, Celine—jealousy isn't very becoming," he said disapprovingly. "I managed to convince the girl that I'm a political prisoner who fights terrorism." William rubbed his chin thoughtfully. "But we're not here to talk about Andrea . . ."

Celine rolled her eyes. "I know—we're here to talk about Princess Pill," she finished unenthusiastically. "Here are Elizabeth's keys." She tossed the key ring on his desk.

William delicately touched the keys with one pale finger. The feel of the jagged metal sent a thrill through him. He imagined Elizabeth carrying them everywhere she went, and feeling lost when she discovered they were missing. "Well done. Have you been keeping an eye on Elizabeth like I asked you?"

"Well, kind of . . ."

"Celine!" William barked at her.

Celine recoiled. "Look, I'm sorry. But I can't stand watching Miss Goody Two-Shoes and her boyfriend Clark Kent fawning all over each other. Spying on them is about as much fun as watching alfalfa grow." She puffed on her cigarette. "But I did find out a few things."

"Like what?"

"She and Tom are still glued to each other's side."

"And?"

Celine chewed her lip thoughtfully. "Oh, yeah, she's working on a project for her Shakespeare class."

"That's it?" William's ice-blue eyes glared at her threateningly. "That's all you have to report?"

"There's not much to tell—Peaches is so squeaky clean," she said, her eyes wide.

"I don't have time to play games," he hissed. "I should have known better than to give you something so important to do. I guess I'll just have to do it myself!"

Celine hopped off his lap and scurried into the corner like an injured animal. William took a small block of wax from his pocket and made several

17

impressions in it with Elizabeth's keys. Then he pulled a volume of Shakespearean sonnets off the shelf. He thumbed through the text and copied a few lines onto a slip of paper. He tried to imagine the surprise on Elizabeth's face when she opened the note. If only he could be there to watch her read it.

When he was finished, he handed the key ring to Celine, along with the note. "Put this in her car. You can leave her keys in the ignition. I'll have some duplicates made tomorrow."

"And what if I don't?" Celine asked testily.

William snatched Celine's cigarette, took one last puff, then smashed it into the tabletop. "Any other questions?"

Celine swallowed hard. "What does the note say?"

William snaked his arm around Celine's waist. "It's poetry. Go ahead and read it if you want, but I guarantee you won't get much out of it." He flashed her a seductive smile. "I'm afraid your talents, Celine, lie elsewhere."

Celine ran her fingers through his hair. "Why, Sir William," she answered sweetly. "You do know how to charm a lady."

Chapter Two

"Bruce! Wake up!"

Bruce opened his eyes. Lila was screaming and pounding on his chest. Her eyes were distant and glassy. *Oh, great,* Bruce thought groggily, *Lila's finally lost it. I'm going to die on this mountain with a maniac.*

He bolted upright, grabbing her firmly by the wrists. "I'm awake! I'm awake! Lila, get ahold of yourself." He looked at her in confusion. "What's wrong?"

Lila pulled away. She stared at him for a moment. "I'm so glad you're OK. . . ." Her voice trembled.

"Why wouldn't I be?" Bruce looked down and saw that he was in his underwear. He glanced back at Lila. She was shaking. "Hey, what's going on here?"

"You don't remember anything?" she said with surprise. Lila's face was pale, as if she'd just seen a ghost.

What is she talking about? Bruce wondered. Lila's

19

strange behavior was starting to worry him. Maybe she really had gone off the deep end. "Remember *what*?"

"The fever," she answered. "You had a high fever. I stayed up last night trying to take care of you, and when you wouldn't wake up just now, I thought you were—" Her voice broke.

Bruce swallowed hard, grateful that she didn't finish the sentence. He had no memory of being sick, and except for a little soreness, he felt fine. He might have thought this was some elaborate trick that Lila was playing out of boredom, but the fear in her eyes told him it was real. "You took care of me last night?" he asked.

Lila nodded. The color was slowly returning to her cheeks. "I tried. I didn't really know what I was doing, but I guess it worked."

Bruce imagined Lila by his side, nursing him back to health. It was too bad he was so knocked out that he hadn't been able to enjoy it. She must have looked beautiful as she wiped the perspiration from his brow and tucked the edges of the blanket underneath him.

Bruce chuckled. He probably didn't look too bad either, with his shirt off. Lila must have loved every minute of it. "Well, I appreciate your taking care of me, Lila. I really do," Bruce said, covering himself with the blanket. "And I just want you to know that I don't blame you for making the most of it."

Lila's eyes narrowed. "Making the most of *what*?"

"You know." Bruce winked flirtatiously. "Taking advantage of the situation." He made a show of flexing his well-developed muscles.

Lila's cheeks turned dark red. Her voice flared in anger. "You never quit, do you?" She gathered up her clothes, snatched the blanket away from him, and stalked off to the other side of their makeshift camp.

"Believe me, I understand why you'd want to play Florence Nightingale," Bruce called to her retreating back. "With a patient as gorgeous as myself, it would be tough for any woman to resist!"

Nina Harper looked into her mailbox. "I can't believe this!" The beads in her hair clicked as she shook her head. "It's empty for the third day in a row!"

Elizabeth opened her book bag and loaded it with the letters and postcards that filled her box. "I keep telling you—the only way to get letters is to write them."

Nina folded her arms across her chest. "I have two papers and a physics exam next week—who has time to write letters?"

"That just depends what your priorities are." Elizabeth slung the book bag over her shoulder. "What's more important—maintaining friendships or your homework?"

Nina laughed. "I'd like to hear you debate that one with my dad." She held open the door for Elizabeth as they stepped out of the student union into the bright sunlight.

Elizabeth squinted and reached for her sunglasses. The sky was a brilliant blue, perfectly cloudless, and a warm breeze was blowing through the campus. It was the kind of day that would usually lift Elizabeth's spirits no matter how bad a mood she was in. But today, it didn't work.

"Is there anything I can do to help?" Nina asked, as though she could read Elizabeth's mind.

Elizabeth shook her head. "I don't think so. Just letting me dump my problems on you was a big help."

"Anytime." Nina put her arm around Elizabeth's shoulders. They sat down on the stone steps of the library. "If you don't mind me asking, what are you going to do?"

Elizabeth shrugged. It was a question she had asked herself a thousand times since she got up this morning, and still she had no answer. "I don't know. What do you think I should do?"

"That's a tough one." Nina shaded her eyes from the sun and stared into the distance. "I guess you'll have to follow Jessica's lead."

Elizabeth leaned back on her elbows. The sun felt warm on her skin, but it couldn't penetrate the chill that was deep inside her. "But what if Jessica doesn't do anything? Then what?"

Nina frowned. "Then you'll have to take matters into your own hands."

"Good morning, ladies!" Tom Watts called as he walked up the path. Nina smiled and waved, while Elizabeth greeted him with a soft, slow kiss on the lips.

Instantly the worry lines on Elizabeth's forehead disappeared. "And how have you been since the last time I saw you?"

Tom scratched his head. "OK, I guess. Not much has happened in two hours." He kissed her again. "Oh, but what a long two hours it's been. . . ."

Nina shook her head in mock disgust. "Throw in a balcony, and you two could make Romeo and Juliet look like a couple of amateurs."

Elizabeth couldn't tear her eyes away from Tom. If there was one person who could make everything right again, it was he. "So when do you want to meet for lunch?" she asked.

Tom's smile faded. "I'm sorry, Liz, I can't. John is sick today, so I have to cover his shift at WSVU."

"Nina?" Elizabeth asked hopefully.

"Sorry." Nina smiled apologetically. "I'm just going to grab an apple. I want to get a jump start on my research paper."

"Why don't we meet tonight?" Tom held Elizabeth's hand. "Maybe we could do a double date with Danny and Isabella. Are you in the mood for a movie?"

Elizabeth sighed. "It sounds great—but I promised my brother that I'd visit him tonight. Besides, I need to break the news about Jessica to him." She gave Tom's hand a squeeze. "Maybe we can go out tomorrow."

"I understand." Tom gave Elizabeth a long, leisurely kiss.

Nina stood up and brushed the dirt off the back of her jeans. "I hate to break up the party, guys," she said as they continued to kiss. "But I've gotta get a move on."

"Bye," Elizabeth said, with a dreamy expression on her face. "I'll talk to you later."

"Bye!" Tom called, just as Nina disappeared into the library.

Elizabeth stood quietly in Tom's arms, holding him tight. Her body felt light, as if she were floating through space, far away from her troubles. It was comforting to know that no matter what problems came her way or how bleak everything seemed, she'd always have Tom.

Jessica didn't want to get up. It was almost lunchtime, and she still hadn't managed to drag herself out of bed. She lay on her back, staring at the white ceiling, trying to think of one good reason to start her day. There were classes she was missing, but there was no way she'd be able to concentrate on a lecture. There were friends she could see, but Jessica wasn't in the mood for conversation. Then of course there was lunch, but she didn't feel like eating.

The phone rang. "Go away," she mumbled at the phone, but it continued to ring. She covered her ears with a pillow to block out the sound. It was funny how annoying a phone could be when it rang endlessly—before today, she'd always picked up the receiver on the first ring.

After the tenth ring, Jessica couldn't take it anymore. She lunged for the phone. "Hello?" she barked impatiently.

"Jess? I'm glad you answered. It's James."

Jessica's body tensed. Her first instinct was to slam down the phone, but she didn't move. The receiver was glued to her ear. "Y-yes?" she responded warily, gripping the phone with both hands.

"I want to see you. I think we need to have a talk. . . ." James said.

Jessica's heart pounded in her chest. He was right—they did need to talk. She needed to tell him just how much he hurt her. But she couldn't do it to his face. Jessica didn't ever want to see him again. "You're right, we do need to talk," she said shakily. "But let's do it over the phone."

There was silence on the other end. Then James finally spoke. "Come on, Jessica. I want to see you. Meet me on the quad in an hour." His voice was edgy.

Jessica pictured James as he said those words, his mouth drawn in a hard line, his eyes gleaming. She felt as though she was going to be sick. "No, James. It's not a good idea."

"In an hour, Jess," he persisted. "Please." A second later she heard a click and a dial tone. He'd hung up.

Jessica slammed down the receiver and clenched her jaw. *What makes him so sure I'm going to show up?* she seethed. She threw off the bedcovers and started to pace the room. *What is so urgent that he has to see me?* she wondered. Maybe he wanted to apologize. James had probably woken up with a killer hangover and a load of regret. *He needs me to forgive him so he can feel better,* she thought angrily. Not a chance. If anything, she'd make sure he'd remember what he had done to her for the rest of his life.

Jessica tore through her closet, looking for something to wear. Balled up in the corner was a wrinkled pair of blue sweats. "The first thing I'll tell him," she said aloud as she jammed her legs into the sweatpants, "is that he drinks too much."

She tied the drawstring on her sweatpants and searched through her dirty laundry for the sweatshirt. Jessica imagined James's face before her, listening to what she was saying. "When someone says that they don't want to do something, don't ignore it!" She threw on the sweatshirt. The anger she had been holding inside felt like a gigantic knot in her stomach that was suddenly unraveling. "You had no right to try to make me do something I didn't want to do!"

It felt wonderful to release some of her anger, but the words were just bouncing off the walls of her room. She could spout off all day, but her words wouldn't mean anything if they didn't reach James's ears. Jessica put on her sneakers. He had to be told.

Looking in the mirror, she noticed the dark circles under her eyes and the tangles in her long blond hair. Jessica quickly ran a comb through her hair, and for an instant she wondered if she should put on a

26

touch of blush to take the paleness out of her complexion. "You look good enough," she said to her reflection, not bothering to open her makeup kit.

Jessica smiled wryly when she thought back to yesterday, and how much time she'd spent getting ready for her date with James. Last night, she had wanted to look like a goddess. Today, she didn't care if she looked like Medusa.

Alexandra Rollins sat alone at a small table in the corner of the dining hall. From where she was seated, she had a full view of the members of the Theta sorority chatting as they ate lunch. Alison Quinn, the sorority's vice-president, was engaged in an animated conversation with the other sisters. Although Alex couldn't hear what she was saying, she could guess by the nasty scowl on Alison's face that she was probably spreading a rumor about someone. Alex's stomach did a somersault. Were they talking about her?

Alex took a bite out of her sandwich and scanned the room. Many of the students in the cafeteria seemed to be paying close attention to the Thetas. Lovesick stares from men and envious glances from women seemed to gravitate toward their table. Even though Alex herself belonged to the prestigious sorority, recently she hadn't really felt comfortable with the popular, perfectly groomed Thetas.

Alex wondered how long it would take for her to feel at home with them again. She had done everything they asked her to do: she had cut down on her drinking and was getting her life back together. Alison couldn't deny that Alex had come a long way from the days when she'd made a habit of passing out at fraternity parties. But still, her sorority sisters weren't exactly showering her with love and support.

Laughter erupted from the Theta table. Alex devoured her sandwich as she struggled to fight back tears of loneliness. *If they don't want me around, why don't they just tell me?* she thought miserably. Although she tried to fight it, her mind wandered to the half-empty bottle of vodka sitting in the back of her closet. Last week she had placed it out of sight— now she realized she should have poured it down the drain instead.

Alex forced herself to focus on something besides that alluring bottle. She had worked too hard on getting her life back on track to throw it all out the window. She looked over at the soda fountain. *I'll have to settle for something else instead,* she decided resolutely. And the soda fountain was near the Theta table. Maybe if she walked by them, someone would talk to her.

Alex smoothed back her hair and stood up straight. She strolled past the table with as much confidence as she could muster. A few of the girls noticed her and gave her a quick smile or mouthed "hi." But the person who counted most, Alison, was too busy talking to notice her.

Alex's shoulders slumped in disappointment. She filled a glass with ice and jammed it angrily under the spout. Why should she care what Alison thought, anyway?

"Hey, be careful with that drink," a voice behind her said jokingly. "We wouldn't want anyone to get hurt."

Alex whipped around to see gorgeous Noah Pearson pointing to the glass in her hand. The last time she had seen him was at a Sigma party, where she'd accidentally spilled a drink all over his shirt.

"Lucky for me," he said good-naturedly as he nodded at the orange liquid that was pouring out of Alex's tilted glass into a puddle at her feet. "The floor got it this time."

Alexandra was mortified. "I'm sorry," she gasped apologetically. "Look at this mess—I spilled orange fizz all over the place."

"What did you just call it?" Noah asked as he mopped up the spill.

Alex was so taken by the way Noah was helping her that she hardly noticed the question. "What?" she said distractedly. "Orange fizz?"

"Yeah, that's it—I've never heard someone call soda 'fizz' before. That's cool." Noah smiled.

Alex started to melt. Noah had the sexiest smile she had ever seen. She'd noticed it the very first day of their psychology class. He seemed so serious, but friendly—saying hello to nearly everyone who passed by him. Whenever the professor asked a question, Noah seemed to know the answer, but he was never a show-off. The first time she'd seen him, Alex wanted to know him better. As she watched him throw away the soaked napkins she wondered dismally what Noah must have thought the first moment he saw her. Probably something along the lines of *There goes a world-class klutz.*

Noah picked up a tray. "Have you started studying for the big psych exam?" he asked.

Alex chewed her lip nervously. She didn't recall hearing about a test. She probably wouldn't even be able to locate her notes, which were buried somewhere in the wasteland of her room. "I hadn't really thought about it," she answered awkwardly. "But I guess I should."

"I was thinking that maybe we could study together," Noah said shyly. "That is, if you want to," he added quickly.

Of course I want to! Alex thought, biting her tongue to keep from saying it out loud. She wanted to jump for joy, but with a serious and smart guy like Noah, it was best to play it cool. "Sure," she said.

Noah smiled. "Great—whenever you're ready, let me know."

"OK, sounds good," Alex said casually, even though she felt as though she was about to burst. Out of the corner of her eye, she looked to see if any of the Thetas had picked up on what had just happened. As far as she could tell, they hadn't. *Oh well, who cares,* Alex thought with a sigh. *Noah Pearson just asked me out on a date—sort of.*

Chapter Three

Elizabeth ate her lunch at a picnic table outside the dining hall. Without Tom and Nina around to lift her spirits, sadness started to creep up on her. She wondered how Jessica was doing. Had she even made it to class? Elizabeth decided she'd better check up on her twin as soon as she finished her lunch.

"Mind if I join you?"

Elizabeth looked up. It was Maia. Her muscles tensed almost immediately. "Sure," Elizabeth said, her voice heavy.

Maia took a seat opposite Elizabeth. "I saw you sitting over here, so I thought I'd come by and see how things turned out last night with Jessica."

Elizabeth pushed away her plate of fruit salad. "Actually, it didn't turn out so well."

The corners of Maia's mouth drooped in a slight frown. Deep furrows appeared above her brow. "What happened?" she asked.

31

Elizabeth took a deep breath. "After you told me about what happened between you and James, I drove up to the Mountain Lodge Inn. They'd already left, so I headed back down, to Lookout Point."

Maia's face paled, her eyes distant. To Elizabeth, it seemed as though Maia had suddenly been transported to the night of her own attack. Her lips were moving slightly, but no words came out.

"Maia, are you OK?" Elizabeth reached for her hand.

Maia looked up. "What happened?"

"James was all over her," she said slowly. "Jessica was pretty bruised—but luckily I got there before . . ." Elizabeth's voice trailed off. "I'm just glad I got there when I did."

Maia's face turned ghostly white. Her hand was clasped tightly over her mouth in horror. "How is she?"

Elizabeth fought to keep her voice even. "Pretty shaken up, but I think she'll be fine."

Several uncomfortable moments passed; neither of them spoke. Tears started to flow freely down Maia's cheeks, and Elizabeth had to look away to keep herself from crying. She stared at a point in the distance, willing her eyes to stay dry.

"I'm so sorry, Liz," Maia sobbed. "This is my fault."

A tear escaped and slid down Elizabeth's cheek. "Don't say that, Maia. James is the one to blame. Not you."

"If I had pressed charges, this wouldn't have

happened!" Maia cried. "But I was too scared."

Elizabeth wondered if Jessica was feeling the same way Maia did when she was attacked. Would she be too frightened to confront James in public? Maybe with Maia's help, she wouldn't be. "Do you think you could sit down and have a talk with Jessica?" Elizabeth asked hopefully. "Since you both had similar experiences, I thought maybe you could help her sort out her feelings."

Maia gasped. "No, Liz, I can't talk to her."

"Why not?"

"Because I feel guilty. I feel responsible for what happened to Jessica." Maia's voice broke. "There's no way I could face her."

"Please, Maia—just think about it. It would mean a lot to Jess," Elizabeth said.

"My mind's made up. I can't do it." Maia stood. "I'm sorry," she said as she walked away.

"Just come with me, Lila," Bruce pleaded. "I have a plan."

"No!" Lila fumed as she continued collecting twigs and branches for a fire. "The last time you had a 'plan,' you nearly drowned yourself. I suppose your next brilliant idea will be to reassemble the plane using tree sap and to make me the test pilot!"

Bruce followed close behind her, picking up pieces of dead wood and tossing them onto the pile. "Stop being so pigheaded. I need you to come with me. I'm serious."

33

"Pigheaded? What an enchanting expression," Lila said sarcastically as she cracked a branch over her knee.

"Please, Lila—"

"You're going to have to go by yourself—I'm staying here!" she shouted. Lila was so furious that she refused to even look in Bruce's direction. He had a lot of nerve asking her for anything after that obnoxious Florence Nightingale comment. Especially since she'd stayed up most of the night taking care of him.

There was no getting through to Bruce Patman, Lila decided. Even a brush with death hadn't fazed him. Well, from now on, she didn't care if he got frostbite all the way up to his neck—she'd let him suffer.

Bruce had been silent for a few long moments. "I need you, Li," he said finally, his voice a whisper.

"Of course you need me! You need me to pick up the pieces when you do something stupid," she snapped.

Bruce grabbed her by the shoulders. "Listen to me," he said firmly. "We've already been here several days . . . I don't know how much longer we can last." His eyes were soft and pleading. "We have to work together. It's going to take trust for us to survive."

Lila threw back her head and laughed bitterly. Bruce Patman was the last person she would have trusted before this whole mess. "Bruce, get real. You were the one who bullied me into flying with you in the first place. *You* were the one who crashed the plane, didn't file a flight plan, and forgot to reload the flare gun. Give me one good reason why I should trust you." Lila turned sharply, ready to storm off, when a branch caught her foot, sending her to the ground. *Just great,* Lila thought miserably as she sat up and rubbed her sore ankle. *Another chance for Bruce to humiliate me.*

But Bruce wasn't laughing. "Here's your reason," he said, handing her a folded piece of paper.

Lila eyed him skeptically and grabbed it out of his hands. "What's this?" she asked, unfolding the paper. It was a map of the area.

"I found it at the bottom of the toolbox in the back of the plane. It must have belonged to the guy who sold me the Cessna." He traced his finger along a red line. "I'm pretty sure this is a road about ten miles from here. And if we follow that road, we should get to this—" His finger circled a tiny square. "A rangers station."

Lila felt her heart start to beat faster as she absorbed Bruce's words. If they could find the road and follow it until they hit the rangers' station, there was a good chance they'd be able to find help. Maybe they could even be home before tomorrow. . . .

Bruce continued to study the red line that represented the road. "I don't know how accurate this map is, but it's our last shot."

Lila's throat tightened, her eyes filling with tears. She didn't want to get too excited, but the thought that they might actually be rescued was overwhelming. It was a slim chance, but it was the first glimmer of hope that Lila had felt in days.

"You saved my life, Lila," Bruce said earnestly. "Now let me save both of ours." He reached out and tucked a loose strand of hair behind her ear.

Lila stared into his dark eyes. In their depths, she saw an openness and honesty she hadn't noticed in all the years she had known Bruce.

Lila gently placed her hand in his.

"I'll get us out of here," Bruce vowed. "I promise."

Noah raced out of the cafeteria, a backpack slung over his shoulder and an apple in his hand. After Alex had said she'd study with him, Noah was suddenly too excited to eat. He also suddenly had the urge to run, as he always did when he was ecstatic.

"Alex said yes . . ." he hummed to himself as he tore down the path. He dodged students who were in his way. "I'm going on a date with Alexandra Rollins," he said, a little louder this time. "Okay, so it's just a study date. Who cares?" A guy had to start somewhere.

For weeks he had wanted to ask her out, but it never seemed like the right time. Several times he'd been on the verge of suggesting they go to a movie or out for pizza, only to have Alex take off in the middle of their conversation. Noah wasn't sure why today had been different—but he really didn't care. She'd said yes.

Noah's jog gradually slowed down to a stroll. His heart pounded and his breathing was heavy. With every breath he exhaled, the initial euphoria began to wear off and reality sank in. Sure, Alex said she'd study with him, but that didn't necessarily mean she'd want to go on a real date. Noah felt a weight pressing down on his shoulders. He had one shot. He couldn't blow it.

Noah took a bite of the crisp apple, his head filling with doubts. Alex was beautiful, intelligent, and sweet. She could probably have any guy she wanted. *Alex is used to dating sports stars, not psychology geeks,* he thought. She had been seeing Mark Gathers before he left school. And Noah had heard that she'd been seen recently with Elizabeth Wakefield's ex-boyfriend, Todd Wilkins. How could he compare?

"Which U.S. state is known as the Pine Tree State?" Danny Wyatt read from the card in his hand. He leaned back on the blanket he and Isabella Ricci had spread out on the grass and watched a few fluffy clouds pass by. It was the perfect day for a picnic.

"Hmmm . . ." Isabella scratched her head. "I'm going to say Maine."

Danny's brown eyes narrowed suspiciously. "You peeked."

"No, I didn't—I swear," she said innocently. "I used to go to summer camp there when I was little." She smiled mischievously. "Does this mean I won?"

Danny sighed. Isabella would be gloating over this for days. "Yes," he muttered under his breath. "You won."

Isabella cupped a hand to her ear. "What? I can't hear you," she teased. She jumped up and did a little victory dance around the blanket.

Danny tried not to laugh as he watched her kick up her heels. It amazed him how she could jump around like a kid and still look beautiful and sophisticated. Everything she did had style. "Don't get too excited," he said dryly. "You had all the easy questions."

"Oh, really?" Isabella raised one perfect eyebrow. "Tell you what, sore sport, I'll bet you double or nothing you can't tell me what special day is coming up next week."

Danny's smile faded. He squinted and rubbed his dark forehead as though he was concentrating. He knew the occasion she was talking about. It was their anniversary. They had been dating for three months. He shrugged. "I'm stumped," he said.

Isabella's lips curved downward into a frown for just a moment before they quickly transformed into a wry smile. "Danny! Cut it out! Be serious."

"All right, all right. Of course I remember, Izzy. How could I forget?" Danny put his strong arms around her shoulders. "Three months ago you became the luckiest woman on campus," he joked.

"Talk about arrogant!" Isabella laughed as she took his arm and twisted it behind his back. "If I'm the luckiest woman, what does that make you?"

"A terrible wrestler?" Danny said breathlessly. Even though he was ten times stronger than Isabella, he pretended that he couldn't break her hold.

"Wrong!" Isabella released her grip. "Honestly, Danny," she said with exasperation. "You don't have a romantic bone in your body."

Danny looked at her with surprise. "What do you mean? Didn't I take you out for a nice romantic evening of bowling last week?"

Isabella rolled her eyes and threw her hands up in the air. "See? This is what I'm talking about."

"But you had fun, didn't you?" He pouted.

"I did until you invited those high school kids to play with us," Isabella said ruefully.

Danny's feelings were hurt. "They looked lonely," he answered defensively.

"All six of them?" Isabella shot back. "Just face it, Danny. You don't know the first thing about romance. I bet you couldn't even plan a romantic evening to save your life."

Danny waved a finger at her. "Romance is in the eye of the beholder. Some people, like myself, consider a night of bowling to be incredibly romantic."

"Sure, it's right up there with monster truck shows."

"You just don't like bowling because you spend the entire time worrying that you're going to break a nail."

Isabella put her hands on her hips. "Well, Danny, if you went to the manicurist once a week like I do, you'd want to take care of your nails too!"

Danny started to laugh so hard, his stomach hurt.

"What's so funny?" Isabella asked. Her gray eyes stared at him. "It's not funny, Danny."

Danny wiped a tear from his eye and tried to control his laughter. "Don't get upset," he said. "I just think it's funny how girlish you are—everything about you is always so neat and perfect. You never get dirty."

Isabella made a face. "I don't see why that's a problem."

"I didn't say it was a problem—it's just that I like to do outdoorsy stuff and you don't enjoy it because the wind might mess up your hair," he said.

"I can't help it; that's just the way I am." Isabella sniffed. "You, on the other hand, could work a little harder." She grinned.

"Oh, yeah?" Danny kissed Isabella sweetly on the lips. "I'm sorry to report that this is as romantic as I get. Take me or leave me."

"No comment," Isabella answered, kissing him back.

Jessica's hands were shaking. She jammed them into the front pocket of her sweatshirt, hoping she didn't look as nervous as she felt. She sat on a bench in the middle of the quad, her head bent toward the ground. She wanted to avoid talking with any of the students who rushed by on their way to class.

"Calm down," she said to herself under her breath. "You are sitting in the middle of campus. People are everywhere. Nothing is going to happen." She took a deep breath. *Maybe he won't show,* she hoped. The thought of James backing out eased the pressure she was feeling. Maybe she wouldn't have to confront him after all. He was already late; if he didn't show up in the next minute, she'd leave.

A pair of brown loafers stopped directly in front of her. Jessica felt a chill run down her spine. She didn't want to look, but her eyes kept moving up, as if they were being pulled by a magnetic force. When she finally reached his face, Jessica trembled.

"I'm glad you showed up," James said as he took a seat next to her. "We need to talk."

Jessica nodded vigorously. "We do," she said quietly. She was surprised by how feeble and hesitant her voice sounded. Where was the strength and anger she had felt earlier? Everything she had to say to James had come out so perfectly and easily when she'd been alone in her room. She'd even rehearsed what she was going to say on her way over here. Now her mind was a blank—the words had completely escaped her.

James leaned forward on the bench, resting his elbows on his knees. He seemed lost in thought—or was he waiting for her to start first? As much as Jessica knew that this was her opportunity to tell him how much he'd hurt her, she couldn't. Her throat felt tight, as if she were suffocating.

Finally James spoke. "First of all, I just want to say that I'm pretty upset about last night. I thought things were going great between us—I don't know why you had to go and mess it up."

Jessica stared at him, unable to believe that she'd heard him correctly. "What are you talking about?" she managed to choke out.

"I'm talking about your sister. If you didn't trust

41

me, you should have said something instead of sending your sister to keep an eye on us."

Jessica was stunned. "But James, I didn't—"

"Don't bother trying to explain," he said. His face was red. "Your sister has a problem—I just hope she's not dangerous." He held his head in his hands, as though he couldn't understand what had happened. "I mean, when she found us—she really pulled out all the stops."

Jessica was wringing her hands inside her sweatshirt pocket. She had imagined that when they met, she would be the one who was angry. Never in a million years would she have guessed that *he* would lay into *her*.

James continued. "The damage done to my car is a real pain, but I can fix the windshield. What *really* gets me mad is that you led me to believe that you wanted to take the next step. You dressed really sexy and were flirtatious—and then all of a sudden you pull a stunt like that."

Stunt? Jessica was so disoriented by his accusations that she couldn't defend herself. A sickening feeling in the pit of her stomach began to spread throughout her whole body. "I don't know what you mean . . ." she said.

James shook his head. "You know exactly what I mean, Jessica. You led me on."

You're wrong, she thought angrily as she tried to fight back the tears. "I didn't. You don't understand—"

"You led me on," he repeated as though he

didn't hear her. "Admit it, Jess. You had no intention of sleeping with me from the very beginning. So why did you pretend? We could have avoided this whole scene."

"What are you saying?" Jessica's voice shook. "You only went out with me because you thought I'd sleep with you?"

James glared at her. "I'm just saying that you weren't being honest." He stood up. "I think you know that. Keep it in mind so the next guy who comes along doesn't go through the same thing I did." James walked away.

Jessica's eyes burned from hot, stinging tears. His words cut her deeply. Was it possible that he was right? Could she have led him on without even realizing it? Jessica drew her knees up close to her chest and hugged herself. Would she ever stop trembling?

Chapter
Four

Elizabeth returned from lunch to find Jessica sitting on the floor, crying. The clothes she had worn the night before were scattered around her, torn into bits. Jessica was holding a pair of scissors.

Elizabeth slipped the scissors out of her sister's hand and gave her a hug. "Tell me what's wrong," she said gently.

Jessica was covered in the red sequins that were once part of the bustier top she'd worn on her date with James. "He said I led him on . . ." she sobbed.

"*Who* said you led him on?"

"James," Jessica answered, trying to catch her breath. "I talked to him."

Elizabeth's blue-green eyes were filled with alarm. "When did you talk to James?" She handed Jessica a tissue.

"A little while ago. In the quad." She blew her

nose. "He wanted to talk. He said it was my fault—I led him on."

Elizabeth clenched her jaw. Where did he get off, badgering Jessica? Elizabeth was becoming more and more convinced that James was completely sick. "You don't believe that, do you?" she said, struggling to hold her anger in check.

Jessica looked at the ripped cloth. "I don't know," she said. "He twisted everything."

Elizabeth held her sister's hand. "I know for a fact that it wasn't your fault," she said. She had been looking for the right moment to tell Jessica about Maia, and now the time had come. "There's something I have to tell you. I probably should have told you this sooner."

Jessica dried her eyes. "What is it?"

"I didn't just happen to come looking for you last night. . . . After you and James left for the restaurant, Maia came by. We had a talk—actually she was warning me." Elizabeth paused for a moment. She wanted to choose her words carefully.

"Maia went out with James," Elizabeth finally continued. "A few weeks ago, James took her to the Mountain Lodge Inn for dinner, and then they went parking at Lookout Point, just like your date—" Elizabeth stopped.

Jessica stared at her sister, her eyes wide. "James attacked her too?"

Elizabeth nodded. "But Maia was raped." The words hung in the air above them. Elizabeth sat

46

there, watching her sister's expression turn from shock to fear to rage as it all slowly sank in.

"If you hadn't been there, he would have raped me too," Jessica said. She threw her arms around Elizabeth. "Thanks for coming after me. . . ."

Elizabeth's eyes began to water. "Don't you see now? It wasn't your fault. James needs help."

"I can't believe this." Jessica threw pieces of shredded cloth into the wastebasket. "He seemed so perfect. I guess I really have a knack for picking men who are trouble."

Elizabeth moved across the room, cleaning up. "Don't say that. It's not your fault. Who would have guessed James had a dark side? He seemed perfect to me, too."

Jessica nodded. "He's so smooth, so polished. It's like he's two different people."

Jessica went to the bathroom down the hall to splash cold water on her face. When she came back, Elizabeth was loading up her book bag, ready to head off to another class.

"What time do you want to go to Steven and Billie's?" Elizabeth asked.

Jessica lay down on her bed. "I completely forgot about that. . . . I don't think I'm going to go."

"Come on, Jess," Elizabeth coaxed. "Getting away from campus might take your mind off what happened."

"No, I don't want to go tonight—but thanks."

"Think it over, anyway," Elizabeth said. She

automatically reached for her keys, but they weren't on the hook. "You're going to be here, right? I still haven't found my set of keys."

"I'll be here," Jessica said as she crawled under the covers.

Lila couldn't feel her legs. Her whole body had grown numb from exhaustion and cold. The first few miles of their hike were almost fun. She and Bruce had joked and talked about what they would be doing if they were in Sweet Valley. But as the forest became more dense and time wore on, they grew quiet.

Lila was trying not to get her hopes up, but she couldn't help but imagine what would be waiting for them when they got home. Warm beds, clean clothes, hot food. She could almost smell the aroma of fresh pesto as they trudged through the woods.

Bruce walked ahead of Lila, snapping branches so they wouldn't be in Lila's way. The best thing about going home would be seeing her family and friends again. Did her parents even know that they had never made it to school? She imagined they'd be beside themselves with worry. If only there were some way she could reach them, just to tell them that they were still alive.

Lila wondered what her friends were thinking, too. Especially Jessica and the other Theta sisters. She pictured what it would be like, returning to school. The Thetas would probably throw her an enormous welcome-home party. They'd all gather in a circle, with Lila in the middle. They'd hang on her every word as she told them about her adventures in the wild.

Lila smiled at the thought. Of course, she'd only tell the most glamorous and fascinating details. And maybe she'd make up a few. *Thank goodness they can't see me now,* she thought as she looked down at her dirty, ripped clothes. *Me, Lila Fowler, the former Countess di Mondicci, hiking through the wilderness.* Her friends would be even more shocked if they could see Bruce, heir to a multimillion-dollar estate, as the tour guide.

Lila continued on, through the path that Bruce was clearing. Dead branches and leaves crunched under her feet with every step. Her ankle was still sore from earlier in the day, when she had twisted it. It was aching with a dull, throbbing pain. Lila didn't know how much longer she'd be able to walk on it.

Bruce stopped. "Look!" he shouted excitedly, pointing up ahead. "I think I see a clearing!"

A burst of adrenaline shot through her body, and Lila felt her numbed senses come alive. Was it true? Had they finally found the road?

Bruce ran ahead. Lila followed at a much slower pace, but jogging as fast as she could, despite the pain. Through the trees, she spotted the clearing. She could almost see her parents and the Thetas standing there, cheering her on. Welcoming her home.

Bruce stopped at the edge of the clearing. His shoulders dropped. Lila gasped for air and walked the rest of the way, trying to catch her breath. "Did you find the road?" she called.

Bruce didn't answer. Lila yelled again, thinking he hadn't heard her. She watched in confusion as Bruce paced back and forth, not saying a word.

When she reached the spot where Bruce was standing, she understood. Her heart felt as though it had sunk to the pit of her stomach. There wasn't a road: instead she saw a sharp drop-off, a cliff of jagged rock. They were standing on the edge of a ravine that looked at least a hundred feet wide and was probably twice as deep.

Bruce swore savagely, hurling wood, rocks, clumps of dirt—anything he could find—off the edge of the cliff.

Lila's vision of home evaporated into thin air. She sat down on a rotting tree stump and covered her face with her hands. Hot tears poured from her eyes.

Celine crossed the parking lot, looking for the space where Elizabeth's Jeep was parked. *My, my, my—what a feminine car,* Celine thought sarcastically. If William was going to make her drive Miss Prissy's car, why couldn't she own something elegant, like a Cadillac convertible? At least then Celine could enjoy herself.

She unlocked the door. Vinyl seats. Yuck. Celine pulled out the note she had tucked into her bra and read it to herself. William was right—she didn't really know what the words meant. Celine laid it on the dashboard.

Now what was she supposed to do? Was she supposed to leave the keys in it—no, she was supposed to bring them back to the room. That wasn't right either. How was she supposed to remember things when William changed his mind as fast as lightning?

It took a few minutes, but Celine finally remembered what she was supposed to do. Something about moving the Jeep into the middle of the lot and leaving it there. . . . That didn't make a lot of sense, but she wasn't about to take the time to figure it out. *It's just like what my granny always says,* Celine thought, *figuring out a man is about as easy as teaching a rattlesnake to talk—and only half as interesting.*

Celine climbed into the driver's seat, which was a lot harder than it looked, especially since she was wearing a mini and three-inch heels. After a bit of a struggle, Celine eventually positioned herself in the car and started the engine. It roared.

"I wonder if William knows that his Fragile Flower drives a tank," Celine said aloud.

Celine reached for the stick shift. She had never driven a standard before. How hard could it be?

She stepped on the clutch and put the Jeep in first gear. *Now what?* William had said something about the little pedal on the right. . . . Celine popped the clutch. The car jerked as the engine stalled. *Did I break it?* Celine wondered. Maybe she could find some cute man to push the car for her. . . .

Celine turned the key again, this time stomping

on the gas. *It's moving!* Celine started to panic. The Jeep lurched forward out of the parking space in a series of spastic movements. She watched as the Jeep rolled closer and closer to the green Jaguar parked in the space opposite. *Turn the wheel!* she said to herself. She cut the wheel just in time, missing the car by inches. The engine died.

"Stupid car!" she shouted at the dashboard. *This would never happen with a Cadillac,* she thought. Celine fanned herself with the note, trying to calm her nerves. She wasn't sure if this was the parking job Willie had in mind, but it would have to do.

So much for a joyride. Celine hopped out, leaving the keys in the ignition. Who cared if the Jeep blocked four other cars? It wasn't her problem. It was Dizzy Lizzy's car. She'd have to take care of it all by herself.

Alex stared at the framed photograph on her desk. It was a picture of her and Mark just before he left to pursue his basketball career. *Why am I hanging on to this?* she wondered. It had been over between them for months. "It's time to move on, Alexandra Rollins," she said aloud. Impulsively Alex grabbed the picture frame and threw it against the opposite wall. It shattered and fell into the wastebasket below. Three points.

Alex opened her closet. Moving on meant taking care of other things as well—like getting rid of the vodka she was hiding in the back of her closet. She grabbed the bottle and a handful of change, and went out into the hallway.

Alex slipped quietly into the bathroom and checked to make sure no one was around. Then she unscrewed the cap on the vodka and poured the alcohol into the sink. She smiled as she watched the clear liquid spiral down the drain. Alex once thought that vodka made her feel good, but looking back, she realized how much happier she'd been since giving it up. Of course, her lifted spirits might have something to do with the fact that she was going to get to spend time with Noah. She threw the bottle in the trash.

Alex walked down to the lobby, where the vending machines were. She popped some change into the machine and pushed a button. As she stood there, her eyes were drawn to an advertisement on the wall for the campus support hot line. She had called several times, and they had always helped her when life was tough. One of the operators who went by the name of T-Squared had helped her through a really bad time. She could talk to him for hours.

Alex scooped up the can of ginger ale and headed back to her room. She had a familiar urge to pick up the phone and call T-Squared, but it seemed silly since everything was going so well. Then again, she was pretty nervous about her study date with Noah. Maybe he could give her a few tips.

When she got back to her room, she reached for the phone.

"Campus hot line," a deep, sexy voice answered.

Alex smiled. It was him. "T-Squared? This is Enid." Enid was Alex's real name, but very few people on campus knew it. The first time she'd called the hot line, she hadn't wanted to give away her real identity.

"Enid—I haven't heard from you in a while. How've you been?" T-Squared asked. It sounded as though he was happy to hear from her.

"Actually, I've had a wonderful day," she said enthusiastically. "There's this cute guy in my class and he asked me out!"

"That's great! Congratulations. How did you get his attention?"

Alex paused for a moment. She was embarrassed just thinking about that orange puddle on the floor of the cafeteria. Even though Alex didn't know who T-Squared was, she didn't want him to think she was a clumsy idiot. "It's kind of humiliating."

"I'm sure it wasn't that bad—what did you do?" he said sympathetically.

Alex's cheeks burned just thinking about it. "I don't want to get into it."

"Hmmm, let's see if I can guess what it was." There was a pause at the other end of the line, as if T-Squared was immersed in thought. "Did you make fun of the clothes he was wearing?"

"No," she answered.

"Did you accidentally set fire to his thesis paper?"

Alex giggled. "No."

"Did you drop a glass jar filled with your prized cockroach collection in the middle of the student union, causing mass hysteria and widespread panic among the students of SVU?"

"No—but close." Alex laughed.

"See? It could have been a lot worse," T-Squared reasoned.

Alex sat comfortably on her bed and opened the can of ginger ale with a loud *snap*.

"What was that sound? You didn't crack open a beer on me, did you, Enid?" he said, his voice filled with concern.

"No, just a can of fizz." She took a sip. "I guess you're right, it could have been a lot worse. But I'm afraid he probably thought I was a moron."

"Wait a minute, didn't you just tell me he asked you out?" T-Squared asked.

"Well, yeah . . ."

"It sounds to me like he's definitely interested. Why would he ask you out if he didn't want to be with you?"

"I know," Alex answered, unable to contain herself. She knew Noah must be at least semi-interested, but she liked to hear someone else confirm it.

"So what are you going to do next?" T-Squared asked.

"I guess I'll give him a call." Her smile quickly faded. "You don't think he changed his mind? Maybe he thinks he made a mistake. . . ."

T-Squared laughed. "No way. With a girl as

terrific as you—he probably sang all the way home."

Alex's stomach did a flip-flop. "What a sweet thing to say!"

"I mean every word of it," T-Squared said seriously. "You're a very special person. He's a lucky guy."

Alex blushed. She hadn't expected such a strong reaction from him. Was T-Squared jealous? It was hard to imagine, but the idea certainly didn't bother her. In fact, she liked it.

Chapter
Five

"Maybe I should have gone to Steven's after all," Jessica said to herself as she flipped idly through a fashion magazine. She glanced at the clock. Only ten minutes had gone by since the last time she checked. This was turning out to be one of the longest days of her life.

Jessica tossed the magazine onto the floor. *I need to do something,* she thought. She had spent almost the entire day cooped up in the room, afraid to bump into James. If only Sweet Valley University were larger—then she'd actually have a shot at going about her normal life without ever having to see him again. Unfortunately the campus was small enough so that Jessica pictured herself having to dodge him for the rest of her college career.

Since she wouldn't leave, Jessica needed some entertainment to come to her. The perfect person to come to her rescue would be Lila. Jessica knew that

Lila had planned to go to a spa with her mother before she came back to school, but even so, she should have been back days ago. Jessica had tried to reach her several times, but it was as if Lila had disappeared into thin air.

Jessica reached for the phone and dialed Lila's number. She let the phone ring several times, but there was no answer. The answering machine didn't even click on. The tape must be full.

Jessica hung up. *Maybe Lila's not coming back at all,* she thought with disappointment. Lila was still trying to get over her husband's death—she probably wasn't ready to get back into college life. Still, she could have called. Didn't she know that everybody at SVU was wondering where she was?

Jessica dialed the Fowlers' mansion in Sweet Valley. If Lila didn't plan to fill anyone in on her plan voluntarily, Jessica would have to search out some answers herself.

Grace Fowler sounded characteristically elegant when she answered the phone. "Hello? Mrs. Fowler? This is Jessica Wakefield."

"Hi, Jessica!" Lila's mother sounded surprised to hear from her. "How are you? Is the semester off to a good start?"

"Yeah, pretty much," Jessica answered, trying to come across significantly more cheerful than she actually felt. "It's hard to get back into the swing of things after Christmas break."

"I remember what college was like. Sometimes it

would take me a whole month just to crack a book—but don't tell Lila that." Mrs. Fowler laughed. "Do me a favor and keep an eye on my daughter for me. Make sure she doesn't fall too far behind."

"I will—as soon as she gets here," Jessica answered. "When is she supposed to come back?"

There was a pause on the other end. "What do you mean? Isn't she at school?"

Jessica was puzzled. Didn't she know where her own daughter was? "I haven't seen Lila since Christmas break—that's why I called. I thought she changed her mind about SVU . . ."

"I just don't understand it," Mrs. Fowler said anxiously. "Lila left several days ago with Bruce Patman. They were flying back to school. Is Bruce back?"

Jessica usually made it her business *not* to know where Bruce was—he could drop off the face of the earth for all she cared. And as far as Jessica knew, Lila felt the same way. Still, Jessica thought back over the past few days. Had she seen Bruce at all? "I don't think he's around," she answered after a few moments.

"There has to be a good reason for this," Mrs. Fowler said. Jessica could hear a tinge of panic in her voice. "You're sure neither one of them is there?"

"Positive," Jessica answered. She was starting to get nervous.

"I'm going to make a few phone calls—to try and figure out what's going on." Mrs. Fowler spoke quickly. "I'll call you back if I hear anything. If you hear from either one of them, call me right away."

"Of course," Jessica answered. There was a click on the other end of the line. Jessica tried to control the fear that was growing inside her. *There has to be a rational explanation for why they're not back yet,* she told herself. But what could it possibly be?

Bruce walked back and forth along the edge of the ravine, trying to discern whether or not they could get across. The sides of the cliff looked fairly smooth, and without equipment it would be incredibly dangerous. *It's not worth the risk,* he decided. *We have to stay here.*

The sound of Lila's sobs made Bruce pause. He looked over to where she sat, hunched up. He kept waiting for her to scream at him, to tell him that he was a total idiot. Her taunts would have been infinitely easier to take than her tears. *Way to go, Patman,* he thought guiltily, *you screwed up again.*

"Hey, it'll be all right," Bruce said, putting his arm tightly around her. "Shhh. Lila, don't cry."

Lila shook her head. "We're not going to make it, Bruce."

Normally Lila was so strong, so optimistic. Seeing her lose hope chilled him to the bone. "Don't say things like that," he said shakily. "Someone will find us."

Lila didn't answer. Her whole body shook as she cried, and Bruce held her close. Each tear weighed down on his conscience. "I'm sorry I let you down, Li," he said thickly. "It was a dumb idea."

"It's not your fault," Lila said.

Bruce stroked her tangled hair. *But it is my fault,* he thought miserably as he watched the last few rays of sunlight disappear behind the mountains.

Elizabeth crossed the dark path that led to the student parking lot. She was looking forward to spending a quiet, uneventful evening with her brother and Billie. A few hours away from campus, watching old movies, was exactly what she needed to lift her spirits.

As she reached the edge of the parking lot Elizabeth saw the bright-yellow bubble lights of a tow truck. The truck was just backing up, ready to hook someone's car.

Where did I park the Jeep? Elizabeth wondered as she scanned the first few rows of cars. Last night when she'd brought Jessica back to campus, she thought she'd parked in her usual area, near the entrance of the lot. But now she didn't see the Jeep anywhere.

Elizabeth paused for a few moments. Had she been so upset last night that she'd parked somewhere completely different? That was when she saw the Jeep. It was in the middle of the lot, and a huge tow truck was backed up near its bumper.

"Wait a minute!" Elizabeth yelled, waving her arms wildly to get the driver's attention. *Why is it parked in the middle of the lot?* she wondered. He continued to back up until the truck bumped the Jeep.

"Is this yours?" a male student shouted, pointing.

"Yes," Elizabeth answered distractedly as she waved at the driver. "Please stop!" she called.

"Your Jeep is blocking my car," the student said angrily. "I've been waiting here for an hour!"

The tow-truck driver jumped out and walked over to Elizabeth. "Is this your car?" he asked her.

"Yes, but I have no idea what it's doing there," Elizabeth answered. "Please don't tow it," she begged. "I'll move it out of the way."

He stuck his hands in his pockets. "I don't know if I can let you do that—"

"Please! It'll only take a second . . ."

He thought for a moment, glancing from her to the Jeep. "I don't think my boss would like that."

The student who owned the car took a step toward them. "Would someone make a decision?" he called. "I'm not going to wait around here all night. I don't care who moves it—just get it out of my way!"

The driver shrugged. "Go ahead and get in," he said. "But pay more attention in the future."

Elizabeth breathed a sigh of relief. "Thanks," she said as she climbed into the Jeep.

She was about to jam the key into the ignition when she noticed that her missing keys were already in it. She looked around the near-empty lot nervously. Who had driven the Jeep?

"I don't understand this," Elizabeth muttered as she watched the tow-truck driver pull out onto the street. She bit her lip, starting the engine quickly.

Then a piece of paper, folded up and propped on

the dashboard, caught her eye. She put the car in neutral and picked it up. Elizabeth unfolded the note. It read:

For I have sworn thee fair, and thought thee bright,
Who art as black as hell, as dark as night.

"Is this some kind of joke?" Elizabeth whispered to herself. First her keys were missing, then her car was moved, and now this. A shiver ran down her spine. Who would do such a thing?

Elizabeth looked down at the words again. Not too long ago she had received some creepy notes, but she always found them in the library or in her room. This was different. Somehow it had to be related to her car.

One possibility suddenly dawned on her. Could it be James? Was he trying to scare her into silence?

He obviously doesn't know me very well, Elizabeth thought angrily as she headed toward Steven and Billie's apartment. Elizabeth clenched the steering wheel until her knuckles turned white. *Go and play all the pranks you want, James,* Elizabeth thought. *You're in for the fight of your life.*

"Can you believe it? She actually said I was unromantic." Danny tossed a toy football to his roommate, Tom. He threw it a little high, and the ball hit Tom on the forehead.

"Ouch!" Tom said.

"Sorry—" Danny laughed.

Tom threw the ball back. "It wasn't the football—I'm talking about what Isabella said to you. That must've hit a real sore spot."

"Kind of," Danny said, squeezing the plastic ball with his hands.

"So what are you going to do about it?"

Danny raised his eyebrows. "There's only one thing I *can* do," he said. "Prove her wrong." He threw Tom a short, tight pass.

"And how do you plan on doing that?" Tom tossed the ball, and it landed in Danny's dirty-laundry basket.

Danny made a face. "Nice, Watts." He left the ball right where it was and leaned back on his bed. "Good question. I guess since I'm 'unromantic,' I'm going to need a little help." He looked pointedly at his roommate.

"How did I get roped into this one?" Tom asked, looking up toward the ceiling. "I don't know what you need my help for—you've always done well in the girls department."

Danny smiled. "But I've always had a real subtle approach. I need to do something so romantic—so over the top—that there's no doubt in her mind that she's wrong. I want to be more like you—you know, all hearts and roses. Sappy."

Tom grinned. "Is that a compliment?"

"You know what I mean," Danny said dryly. "Any suggestions?"

"How about a bouquet of her favorite flowers or a bracelet?" Tom suggested.

Danny sighed. "Too common. C'mon, work with me."

"Not sappy enough for you? Let's see." Tom rubbed his temples. "What about taking her to a romantic restaurant? That would be pretty cool."

Danny gave him a thumbs-down sign. "I expected more from you, Tom. Think big."

"Hey, why am I doing all the work? Maybe Isabella's right about you . . ."

"I am working. I'm weeding out your bad ideas," Danny answered. "Think *big*. What's the most romantic date you've had with Elizabeth?"

Tom's eyes were distant, and he smiled. "We went to this little Chinese restaurant that had the most gorgeous view of the city. When Elizabeth went to the ladies' room, I tucked a little note into her fortune cookie."

"What did it say?" Danny asked.

"*I love you*. Afterward we went dancing."

Danny clapped. "I knew you wouldn't fail me, Tombo!"

"Wait a minute—you can't use that. It's copyrighted!"

Danny picked the football out of the laundry basket. "Then may I ask permission to use a variation of that romantic date?"

"No!" Tom said. "I'm not going to cheapen a special memory by allowing you to use it."

65

"What if I said I'd treat you to a double order of atomic nachos?" Danny threw the ball at Tom. "Then would you let me?"

Tom grabbed the ball and thought for a moment. "With extra jalapeños?

"The works."

"OK, big guy," Tom said. He aimed the ball squarely at Danny's chest. "The date is yours."

Steven Wakefield opened the door to his apartment. "Come on in, Liz," he said. "The movie is all set to go, and Billie's eaten most of the popcorn."

Elizabeth waved to her brother's girlfriend. "I'm sorry I'm late—I had a little car trouble."

"There's soda in the fridge," Steven said as he took a seat next to Billie on the couch. "Hey, where's Jess?"

"Jessica isn't feeling too well tonight," Elizabeth answered, helping herself to a can of diet cola.

Billie looked concerned. "Is she all right?"

Elizabeth cracked open the can and plopped down on a chair. "Physically, yes. But emotionally—that's another story."

"She's still upset about Mike, right? It's going to take some time for her to adjust to not being married anymore," Billie said.

Elizabeth took a drink from the can. "It's not about Mike. It's someone else."

"I'm afraid to ask." Steven sighed. "You two are going to make my hair turn gray before my twenty-fifth birthday."

"What happened?" Billie asked.

"Jessica's been dating this new guy," Elizabeth said, her expression serious. "When they were out last night, he assaulted her—I think he would have raped her if I hadn't shown up."

Billie and Steven sat in stunned silence. The next instant Steven was on his feet, pacing the living room of the apartment. His fists were clenched. "What's this creep's name?"

"Steven, honey, please relax. Acting like a madman isn't going to solve anything," Billie pleaded. She turned to Elizabeth. "Poor Jessica. She must be having a terrible time dealing with this."

"It's been really rough on her," Elizabeth said.

Steven continued pacing, his face red with anger. Wasn't there a limit to how much trouble one girl could get into? "I swear, that sister of mine . . . where on earth does she get these guys?"

"It's not her fault, Steven," Elizabeth said defensively. "I've met this guy. He's clean-cut and very polite—at least, I *thought* he was. Even you would have approved."

"If I ever get ahold of that guy . . ."

"Steven!" Billie cried. "Just stop it! There are better ways to handle this than punching some guy's lights out."

Steven sat down. He knew that getting into a fist-fight wasn't the brightest idea, but it might make him feel better. "What's Jessica going to do about this?"

Elizabeth shrugged. "Nothing right now. I was

hoping you two could help me change her mind."

Billie put her arm around Elizabeth. "We'll do anything we can to help. Just let us know what our next move should be." She picked up the empty popcorn bowl and took it into the kitchen.

"That's the problem," Elizabeth said, fixing her gaze on the blank television screen. "*I* don't know what to do. I guess the best thing would be for her to press charges. But there isn't a lot of time."

"I think she has up to three years to report it," Steven said. "But the longer she waits, the tougher it will be to prove."

"It's not just that—I'm worried about the other women on campus. He's done this before."

"Are you serious?" Steven said with surprise. "If you have another victim, then the case will be a snap."

"Not exactly," Elizabeth said. "She won't talk."

Steven leaned back. "I swear, I can't handle you two being in college for four years. Maybe the only solution is to lock you both up in your dorm room and have you watch your classes on closed-circuit TV," Steven teased.

Elizabeth smiled. "You sound more and more like Dad all the time."

"Which reminds me," Steven said seriously. "Are we going to tell Mom and Dad?"

Elizabeth thought for a moment. "I don't know. That's probably Jessica's call." She heard the hum of the hot-air popper coming from the kitchen. "I doubt she'll want to discuss it with them, though.

She's not exactly broadcasting the news."

Billie came out of the kitchen, holding a bowl heaped with popcorn. "Fresh popcorn, anyone?" Steven and Elizabeth reached hungrily for the bowl.

"Does anyone still feel like watching the movie?" Steven asked.

"I could use a little escape from reality," Elizabeth answered. "What did you rent?"

"*Casablanca,*" Billie said.

"Oh, good. If anyone can keep my mind off this mess, it's Humphrey Bogart."

Noah read the same sentence over again for the fifth time. He closed his textbook and leaned back in his chair, unable to concentrate on his work. Even though he still had quite a bit of reading to do before the psychology exam, his mind was somewhere else.

A petite woman with short black hair walked by his study carrel. Noah watched her as she searched for a book in the stacks. *Could that be her?* he wondered. Nearly every girl he saw on campus made him ask that same question. He constantly had an urge to run up to some random girl and say, "Hi— I'm T-Squared," and then she would say, "I'm Enid."

You're crazy, he chided himself. *Certifiably nuts.* How could he be so obsessed with someone he had never even met? Especially when there was Alex. He was still incredibly excited about getting to know her. But there was something so intriguing about Enid—she was a mystery.

Noah saw that the woman with the short black hair seemed to be having trouble locating a book. She went to one of the library assistants for help. The assistant calmly explained to the woman that the book she was looking for had already been taken out by someone else. The girl became very upset and started yelling. Noah shook his head. He was certain that she couldn't be Enid. Enid wouldn't have acted that way.

Get a grip, Pearson, he thought, bringing himself back to reality. *You're not acting like a professional.* Noah's dream was to be a psychologist, and if he wanted to be a good one, he'd have to start learning how to keep himself from getting personally attached to the people he was helping. Even if they were as wonderful as Enid.

His mind drifted off again, back to their phone conversation earlier in the day. As much as he hated to admit it, he'd felt a slight twinge of jealousy when she had told him about the guy she was interested in. She said he was cute, and she seemed to like him a lot. She'd been a bit insecure, so he tried to build her up. By the end of the call he had somehow convinced her to pursue the guy, even though his advice went against everything he felt.

Noah sighed. As much as he disliked talking with Enid about her romantic troubles, he was happy to be helping her in other aspects of her life. For example, since they had been talking, she seemed to have stopped drinking. Even today, instead of having beer, she drank fizz.

Fizz? It was strange how he had never heard any-one use that word, and suddenly he heard it twice in the same day. First from Alex at lunch, and then Enid.

Maybe I have a strange attraction to girls who use the word fizz. He chuckled to himself. Or maybe Enid and Alex came from the same part of the coun-try, where that was a common expression. They might even know each other. It was a distinct pos-sibility. *Maybe Alex can introduce me to her. . . .*

Noah bolted upright in his seat as a startling real-ization shot through him. Could it be possible? Were Enid and Alex the same person?

"What's this?" Jessica asked, staring at the box on her desk.

"A little something to cheer you up," Elizabeth said.

Jessica lifted the lid. Inside the box were eleven custard-filled doughnuts, covered with chocolate glaze. "Oooh. My favorite." She pointed to a vacant space. "What happened to that one?" she asked.

"It didn't survive the trip," Elizabeth said, licking her lips. "So much for the eternal diet."

"You deserved it," Jessica said, reaching into the box. "Listen, you haven't seen Lila or Bruce around, have you?"

"Not since we've come back from break. Why?"

Jessica opened their mini refrigerator and poured herself a glass of milk. "I called Lila's house tonight because I haven't seen her since we were home. Her mom said that Lila left for school about a week ago

71

with Bruce. They were supposed to fly in his new plane."

Elizabeth's brow wrinkled. "Lila and Bruce traveling together? Wow. I didn't think their egos could both fit in a two-seater."

Jessica pursed her lips. "Don't joke around, Liz. I'm worried. What if something happened to them?"

"I'm sure they're both fine," Elizabeth said nonchalantly. "You know how they are. Halfway here they probably had a craving for tacos and decided to fly to Mexico instead."

"I hope you're right," Jessica muttered.

"Unless, of course, they fell madly in love with each other and headed to Las Vegas for a quickie wedding. Can you imagine Bruce and Lila married?" Elizabeth reached for a bite of Jessica's doughnut.

Jessica shook her head. "Now, *that* would be funny." Elizabeth was probably right. Bruce and Lila must have gotten sidetracked—they were both known to pull some crazy stunts.

"Steven and Billie say hi," Elizabeth said.

Jessica took a bite of doughnut. "What movie did you see?" she asked through a mouthful.

"*Casablanca*. Billie and I cried our eyes out, and Steven fell asleep, as usual." Elizabeth had a sip of milk from Jessica's glass. "I hope you don't mind, but I told them about what happened."

Jessica put her doughnut aside. She'd suddenly lost her appetite. "I guess not. It's better than telling them myself."

"Steven said that if you plan to press charges, you have up to three years," Elizabeth said. "But the sooner, the better."

"You've got to be kidding, Liz. I can't do that." Jessica dreaded the thought of seeing James around campus, much less in a courtroom. Not to mention the uproar it would cause. The last thing she needed was to have everyone talking about her. And possibly taking James's side.

"I know it would be tough, but I think if you and Maia worked together—"

"No way," Jessica interrupted. "Let's drop it, OK?"

"But we can't drop it," Elizabeth persisted. "What if James does this to someone else?"

Jessica's stomach felt queasy. She was frightened at the thought of what he could do to any one of the women on campus, but making a public accusation absolutely terrified her. Jessica looked at her sister, her eyes pleading. "It's over. Please, let it go."

Chapter Six

The door to Sigma House opened a crack, and Elizabeth saw the cold, hard eyes of Peter H. Wilbourne III staring back at her. He looked shocked to see her at first, but then his expression melted into a twisted grin. "Well, look who we have here," he snarled.

I can't believe I'm here, Elizabeth thought. She never imagined she'd come alone to Sigma House, much less voluntarily speak to Peter Wilbourne. In her investigation for WSVU, Elizabeth had uncovered a secret society on campus and discovered that Peter was a member. She hadn't been surprised that Peter was involved, but it had been a shock to discover that her boyfriend, William White, was the leader. They both kidnapped her and brought her to Sigma House. Fortunately Tom helped her escape, and together they exposed the society. Even though everything turned out fine in the end, the sight of Sigma House always filled her with terror.

"I'd like to speak with James," Elizabeth said firmly, ignoring the threatening look in Peter's eyes. Judging from the way he stood, with his body wedged in the doorway, he had no intention of letting her in.

"What do you want to see James for? Did you uncover another 'scandal' at SVU?" His laugh was menacing.

Elizabeth glared at him. There was no way she was going to let someone as vile as Peter Wilbourne intimidate her. "Let me in."

Peter shook his head. "Not so fast, Wakefield. James isn't even here."

Just as Elizabeth was about to ask where she could find him, a voice came from behind the door. "Did I hear my name?" James appeared next to Peter. "Oh, Elizabeth, how nice of you to stop by. Please, come in." Elizabeth couldn't quite tell if he was being sarcastic or if he really meant what he'd said.

Peter scowled. Elizabeth tried to walk in, but Peter still blocked the doorway. "It's not over, Wakefield," he hissed.

James tapped him on the shoulder. "Get out of the way, Peter. I'll handle this." Peter turned around and stormed up the stairs.

Elizabeth walked in. On the main floor of Sigma House was a large living room with a few chairs and several ugly plaid couches. There was an enormous television set in one corner and a stereo system in the other. The floor was covered with papers, empty bottles, and takeout boxes.

"Have a seat," he said. James took a pizza box off the couch and threw it onto the floor.

Elizabeth sat down. It was amazing how collected James was today. In his khaki pants and an oxford shirt, with clear, sparkling eyes, James barely resembled the drunken animal she'd seen at Lookout Point.

He sat down. "I assume you're here to apologize?"

"No." Elizabeth snapped. *Stay cool,* she told herself. "I want an apology from you."

James laughed. "You want me to apologize? For what? For not letting you total my car?"

"For what you did to my sister!" Elizabeth shouted. She clenched her teeth.

James was calm. "Look, Elizabeth—your sister is a grown woman who can take care of herself. It's time you stay out of her life."

Elizabeth's anger was rising like a gigantic tidal wave, threatening to crash at any moment. "Listen, if you're the one sending her those notes, stop! It's over between you two, so just leave her alone."

James ran his fingers through his hair. "Notes? What notes? What are you talking about?"

Elizabeth felt the wave of anger exploding over her. "I'm not going to sit here and play cat and mouse with you, James. Just consider yourself warned."

James clenched his fists. "Maybe you should find something else to do besides sticking your nose where it doesn't belong. You Wakefields are so uptight!"

Elizabeth stood to leave. "Your idea of fun makes me sick." She headed for the door.

"Yeah, whatever," James grumbled. "Tell your sister it's over between us. She had her chance and she blew it. She'd better not come crawling back."

"Don't bet on it!" Elizabeth shouted as she slammed the door behind her.

"If everyone's ready, I'd like to start," said Magda Helperin, the president of the Thetas.

The sorority sisters had gathered in the parlor of Theta house. It was a larger crowd than usual—it seemed as though everyone had been able to make it to the meeting. Isabella and Denise Waters moved the coffee table into the dining room so people could sit on the floor. Jessica took a seat on the couch next to Magda.

Once everyone was settled, Magda called the meeting to order. "As some of you know, this emergency meeting is about Lila, who still hasn't returned from Christmas break. Has anyone seen Lila or heard from her?"

Jessica glanced around the room. Everyone was quiet.

Mariela Winterson spoke up. "Did anyone call her parents? Maybe she's still home."

"Jessica checked it out already—she's not there," Magda answered. A look of concern clouded her hazel eyes. She motioned to Jessica. "Why don't you tell them about it?"

Jessica nodded. "I called Lila's house yesterday and I talked with her mother." She cleared her throat.

"Mrs. Fowler said that Lila and Bruce left for school the day before the semester began. They were supposed to fly back to school in Bruce's new plane."

"Bruce isn't back yet either," added Kimberly Schyler, who was dating one of the Sigmas.

A hush fell over the room.

"Mrs. Fowler called me back this morning. She said that the airport had no flight plan on record. But they were going to send a search helicopter just in case." Everyone stared at Jessica, then suddenly all the girls started talking at once.

"Listen up." Magda clapped lightly to calm everyone down. "I know it looks bad, and you're all thinking the worst, but we have to try to be positive. There could be any number of reasons why they aren't back yet. I was hoping we could come up with some ideas about what to do."

Alison Quinn waved at Magda to get her attention. "I spoke with several Sigmas, and they told me they'd be willing to help us with anything we wanted to do. They were thinking of splitting up into groups and showing pictures of Bruce and Lila to people in nearby towns. Maybe someone can give us a clue."

"How about running a piece on WSVU?" someone suggested.

Magda turned to Jessica. "Your sister works there—do you want to check into it?"

"Sure," Jessica said. Anxiety swept over her as she watched the Thetas react to the news. They all looked as alarmed as she felt. Before, Jessica thought she was just overreacting. But now she could see that the situation was as serious as she thought.

After an hour of brainstorming and discussion, the Thetas came up with a game plan. First they would mount a campus campaign with posters and news spots on WSVU to find out if anyone had seen or heard from Bruce and Lila. Then they would search nearby towns, talk to local people, and put up posters. It was a simple plan, and there was a good chance that they wouldn't find anything, but the Thetas all agreed that it was better than sitting around, waiting for something to happen.

"So we'll meet on the quad tomorrow to start spreading the word around campus. Does anyone have anything else to add?" Magda asked. The room was silent. "In that case, the meeting is adjourned."

The circle of Thetas broke and the women mingled, talking about Lila and nibbling on pastries.

Jessica sat on the couch, ignoring the commotion around her. Worrying about Lila had made her temporarily forget about James, but now that the meeting was over, her thoughts returned to him. She dreaded the walk back to her dorm room, afraid that she might bump into him.

"Chocolate-chip cookie for your thoughts," Isabella said, thrusting a dessert plate under Jessica's nose.

"Thanks," Jessica said absently, taking the cookie. She continued to stare out the window.

Isabella plopped down on the couch beside her. "Ahem." She cleared her throat to get Jessica's attention. "I don't recall saying that cookie was free—you still have to tell me what's on your mind," she teased.

Jessica slowly came out of her trance. "I'm sorry I'm so spaced out. A lot has been going on lately." She paused. She'd told Isabella last night that she'd broken up with James, but she'd been vague about why.

And now certainly wasn't the right time or place to go into details. "So how are things going with you and Danny?" she asked to change the subject.

"Pretty well," Isabella said with a sigh. "Our three-month anniversary is coming up." She ate a piece of the cookie. "You wouldn't happen to know anything about where I could buy some camping equipment?"

Jessica shook her head. "I don't have a clue about tents and lanterns, but if you need help picking out the right camping *outfit*, I'm your woman."

A loud shriek from the other side of the room made Jessica and Isabella look up.

"You have a date with *who*?" someone asked Mariela Winterson.

"James Montgomery," she answered, her voice low.

Did she say James Montgomery? Jessica wondered. That couldn't be right. How could he go out with someone so soon after what happened? *I must be imagining things. . . .*

"Did you hear that, Alison?" one of the Thetas shouted. "Mariela has a date with James Montgomery."

81

Dozens of eyes turned to stare at Jessica. Mariela angrily mumbled something to the girl who shouted. Jessica's cheeks began to burn.

"I'm sorry, Jess," Isabella whispered in her ear. Jessica sat on the couch, completely paralyzed. The room was absolutely quiet—it was almost as if they expected her to say something. What did they expect her to do—fight for James?

I have to do something, Jessica thought. She couldn't let one of her sorority sisters go through what she had. Jessica needed to warn Mariela—to tell her that James was dangerous. Mariela might not believe her, but it didn't matter. She couldn't let him do it again. She couldn't sit by and watch it happen.

"Mariela, can I talk with you for a minute?" Jessica asked.

"Sure," Mariela answered, following her into the kitchen. The Thetas gradually resumed their conversations, although their attention seemed to be focused on what was happening in the kitchen.

"I'm sorry you had to hear that," Mariela said. "I didn't mean to embarrass you."

"That's all right," Jessica said. *How am I going to tell her?* she wondered. Her stomach started to ache. "Mariela, I don't think you should go out with James."

Mariela looked at Jessica, her eyes filled with suspicion. "Why not?" she asked. Jessica could tell from the tone in her voice that the other girl thought she was jealous.

"He's not like he seems. He could really hurt you." Jessica put her hand on Mariela's shoulder.

Mariela's eyes narrowed. "Why are you doing this?" she asked. "Are you still in love with him? Is that it?"

Tell her about the attack. "I was never in love with him. I'm just trying to keep you from getting into trouble. That's all." Jessica tried to persuade herself to tell Mariela the truth, but the words wouldn't come.

Mariela shook Jessica's hand off her shoulder and folded her arms across her chest. "James told me you'd do this. He said you'd try to talk me out of going out with him."

"What's going on in here?" Alison Quinn asked as she strolled into the kitchen with an empty platter. It was obvious she'd been listening to the whole conversation.

"Nothing," Mariela said haughtily. "I was just leaving."

"Just think about what I said," Jessica added as Mariela strode out of the room. But it was too late— Mariela's mind was made up and there was nothing she could do to change it.

Where is he?
Noah was late for their study date. Alex had stood outside the coffeehouse for more than half an hour, watching groups of people come and go. Many of them seemed to look at her with pity. She imagined them saying, *Just go home. He's never going to show.*

Alex picked pieces of lint from her flower-print skirt and smoothed the wrinkled pages of her notebook. It had taken an hour of searching, but she'd finally managed to locate her psychology notes under the radiator in the corner of her room. *He must've changed his mind,* she thought sadly.

"I'm so glad you're still here," a voice called to her from behind. Alex's stomach fluttered as she turned around. It was Noah.

"It's a good thing you came when you did. I was just about to go," Alex answered. *He's here,* she thought excitedly. It wasn't her imagination. He was standing right in front of her.

"I'm sorry I'm so late," he panted. He looked a little sweaty, like he must have raced across campus. "I had to help someone with something."

"That's all right," Alex said shyly. "You're here now. That's the important thing." She smoothed her hair nervously, hoping she looked all right.

"I brought a few extra books that I got from the library. I think they might help us study for the exam." Noah showed her the stack.

Alex's jaw dropped. Noah had done all this extra research, and she had barely read the assignments. *He's going to think I'm an imbecile,* Alex worried.

"Shall we go inside?" Noah asked.

Alex nodded. "Sure." She tried to relax by taking a deep breath, then slowly exhaling. It was a trick that T-Squared had taught her. She felt a little better. *Don't be nervous,* she told herself over and over again. Besides, what did she have to lose? She had already embarrassed herself several times in front of Noah. How could it possibly get any worse?

An hour later, Alex knew she was in trouble. Noah could talk about left-brain versus right-brain cognition and Carl Jung's theory of synchronicity as easily as if he were talking about the weather. Alex, on the other hand, had no clue about what he was saying. She realized that she had little hope of passing the exam.

Alex sipped her iced cappuccino as Noah spoke. *Why is he wasting his time?* she wondered. *I'm a lost cause.* She wished she had studied more so that she could impress him with her own knowledge; instead, she was just sitting there, mute.

Noah's soft green eyes lit up as he spoke about psychology. Alex found his passion for the subject irresistible. He reminded her of how she used to feel about learning. It had been a long time since she felt that strongly about anything—especially academics.

"Alex—are you there?" Noah said, waving a hand in front of her face.

Alex snapped out of her trance, chagrined. "I'm sorry. What did you say?"

"I was wondering if you believe that the I Ching is a supernatural entity in itself or that it works through psychokinesis."

Alex tried to think of a way to answer without looking dumb. *It's too late for that,* she thought. What was the I Ching anyway? "Either one sounds good to me," she mumbled.

Noah smiled. "What's wrong? You seem a million miles away."

Alex stared at the enormous pile of books on their table. "I'm just a little lost. There's no way I'm going to be able to pass this test."

"Sure you are," he said confidently. "Hang on a minute, and I'll show you something." He began to draw a diagram to illustrate his point.

Alex sighed. He was so patient and understanding. Noah made her feel so comfortable. She had even been able to admit that she didn't know anything about the material, and he hadn't blinked an eye. He was perfect.

I can't wait to tell T-Squared about this, Alex thought. He had told her that everything with Noah would turn out fine, and so far, it had.

"Take a look at this." Noah turned the chart around so she could see. "Does it make any sense?"

Alex studied the diagram. Much to her surprise, it did make sense to her. Maybe she wasn't such a lost cause after all. "Have you ever thought about teaching?" she asked. "You have a gift for it."

Noah blushed. "I don't know. Sometimes I think about it. But I really want to concentrate on doing research." He turned the paper over. His expression became serious again. "Now let me show you how the other theory relates to this one."

While Noah was drawing, Alex's thoughts wandered to T-Squared. It had been barely twenty-four hours since she'd spoken with him, but she already missed him. She could think of a hundred things she wanted to tell him.

Noah held up the piece of paper. "How about this one?"

Alex smiled. "It's a real work of art."

"Can I help you, ma'am?"

Elizabeth walked into the WSVU station. "I'm sorry—I'm looking for a brilliant, charming journalist, but I can see that I'm in the wrong place." Elizabeth turned on her heel, pretending to head for the door.

"Not so fast," Tom said, wrapping his arms around her. "Are you sure you don't want to take another look?"

Elizabeth glanced around the room in mock seriousness. "No, I'm sure he's not here."

Tom turned Elizabeth around and gave her a passionate kiss.

Elizabeth smiled and looked into his eyes. "Of course, I could always settle for a slow-witted, vaguely handsome campus reporter. . . ."

Tom held her tightly. "I know where you can get one of those." He laughed.

Elizabeth returned his kiss. It felt so good to be

in Tom's arms. When she was with him, nothing else mattered. For one brief, blissful moment, all her cares slipped away.

"So how are things with the Wakefields?" Tom asked.

Elizabeth felt herself being reluctantly dragged back to reality. Why did perfect moments have to end? "Not much different. Jessica's still in a funk. She doesn't want to talk about what happened—she just wants to forget about it." Elizabeth frowned. "But *I'm* not going to forget about it." Her voice was filled with determination. "I just had a run-in with James Montgomery."

"Where?" Tom pulled away and looked into her eyes.

Elizabeth gave him a small smile. "Sigma House."

Tom looked concerned. "You didn't go over there by yourself, did you?"

She nodded. "I wasn't thinking. I was just so mad—"

"Promise me you won't go over there again—at least not without me." He held her hand.

"I promise," Elizabeth said.

"So what did the slimeball have to say for himself?" Tom asked.

"Absolutely nothing. He blames everyone but himself. I don't think he even realizes what he's done." Elizabeth's eyes were hard. "This just confirms everything I've thought about James— he's dangerous. I'm not going to let him get away with what he did to my sister."

"You're right, he *is* a threat," Tom said calmly. "But what are you going to do? You can't force Jessica to press charges if she doesn't want to."

"I know." Elizabeth broke free from his embrace and began to pace the floor of the WSVU station. "I just hate to think that this whole thing could get swept under the carpet. There must be *something* I can do."

"Wait a minute." Tom's face lit up. "You just reminded me of something." He shuffled through the papers on his desk. "I was reading the U of O's campus newspaper this morning to get some idea of the hot news at other schools, and I came across this article. . . . Here it is." Tom pulled the paper from the pile and handed it to her.

Elizabeth read the headline out loud. "'Take Back the Night' March Raises Awareness." She glanced at Tom.

"Go ahead, read it," he encouraged.

Elizabeth scanned the article.

The U of O Women's Group recently organized a rally for victims of crimes against women. The women shared their experiences in the candlelight march and offered support to one another. "It's an empowering experience for women," said Lisa Myers, president of the Women's Group. "I know of many victims who are afraid to leave their rooms after dark. Hopefully we can give them the strength they need to regain control of their lives. To 'Take Back the Night.'"

"U of O isn't the only school doing this sort of thing," Tom said. "People are doing marches like this all over the country."

Elizabeth sat down. "This might be exactly what Jessica needs. Maybe it could even give her enough confidence to come forward."

"There's still a chance that she won't go public, but at least it will bring the issue to light," Tom said. "And Jessica will realize she's not alone."

"Right!" Elizabeth answered enthusiastically. For the first time since the attack, she didn't feel entirely helpless. They were finally going to take action. "Do you think we could have a camera crew at the march? A segment on the WSVU news would really get the exposure we need."

Tom nodded. "Sure. I could report live if you want. That is, unless you think my slow wit and vaguely handsome face would ruin the piece," he joked. "I could always get a replacement, if you prefer."

Elizabeth smiled dreamily and kissed his cheek. "Not in a million years."

Chapter
Seven

"Well, I guess this is it," Bruce said grimly, igniting a small pile of leaves and twigs. "Our last match."

Lila tossed a branch into the flames. It was one of the few pieces of wood they'd managed to find that was actually dry enough to burn. "Do you think it will last the night?" she asked, anxiously watching the fire.

"I hope so," Bruce answered. His expression was somber.

Lila dreaded what the night would bring. What if it snowed, putting out the fire? Lila wondered what it was like to freeze to death. She had heard that it was like drifting off to sleep. They would just fade away. Lila never imagined that was how her life would end. She thought of her husband's last moments. Tisiano had died in a fiery explosion—much like the way he'd lived his life. Part of her wished that she too had been on that Jet Ski when it went up in flames. At least it had been quick. Lila and Bruce would have time to think about the end—time to wait for death to approach. Lila shuddered and started to cry.

Bruce huddled next to her, covering both of them with the blanket. "Don't lose hope," he said soothingly. "We're still here, aren't we?"

Lila wiped a tear from her cheek. "I wish I was as confident as you are."

"The only way we're going to get through this is to keep our spirits up." Bruce attempted a smile. The glow of the fire softened his features and made his eyes sparkle. "I wonder what's happening at SVU right now. Do you think anyone misses us?"

"I'd hope so," Lila said wistfully. Her face brightened a little. "I wouldn't be surprised if our parents sent the National Guard to look for us."

Bruce laughed. "Well, if they have sent scouts, they'd better get here soon. I'm starved." Lila nodded, and Bruce went on, "I'm so hungry, I'd even eat that sludge they serve in the cafeteria."

Lila made a face. "I don't know if I'm *that* desperate." The sights and smells of home suddenly seemed very vivid to her. She was actually beginning to relax. "What's the first thing you're going to do when you get back to campus?"

Bruce thought about it for a moment. "Just before break, I ordered a Limited Edition Jeep Cherokee with some of my inheritance money. I think I'll pick it up from the dealership, then maybe head down to the beach."

Lila closed her eyes and tried to remember what it felt like to lie on the beach and soak up the sun's rays. A cold gust of wind blew, and Lila's dream of the beach evaporated. "What about you?" Bruce asked.

Lila thought for a moment. "I just want to see my friends—and maybe fit in a shopping trip or two." Lila tried to feel excited—to anticipate all the things that waited for them at home—but it felt too distant. Here they were, lying in the dirt with nothing to eat, and they were talking about cars and shopping. Their lives didn't seem real anymore. It was like they were talking about someone else.

"Can you believe it? The computer says there are thirty books in this library on Shakespeare's sonnets, and *all* of them are checked out!" Maia said in frustration.

"Hmmm . . ." Elizabeth answered distractedly. She was busy studying a note that she found slipped under the door earlier in the day. It was in the same handwriting as the note she'd found in the Jeep:

> *For thy sweet love rememb'red such wealth brings,*
> *That then I scorn to change my state with kings.*

Lately, her experience with Shakespeare hadn't been the best. The more Elizabeth thought about it, the less she believed James could be behind the notes. Poetry wasn't exactly his style.

"This is what happens when you wait until the last minute," Maia pouted.

"Shakespeare is a popular guy," Elizabeth said, tucking the note into the pocket of her jeans. "Maybe someone returned a book and they just haven't had a chance to put it back on the shelves yet. I'll go ask."

"Good thinking, Liz. I can see you're not an investigative reporter for nothing," Maia said. "In the meantime, I'll try to find someone in our class who we can bribe."

Maia walked off. Elizabeth saw the new library worker pass by in his wheelchair, replacing books on the shelves. He always gave her the creeps, but she didn't have much choice about speaking to him. "Excuse me, sir," she said.

The man turned around. An expression of complete surprise came over his face. "Yes?" he said, slightly out of breath.

"I'm sorry," she apologized. "I didn't mean to startle you."

"That's all right." He smiled. "What can I do for you?"

"I'm looking for a copy of Shakespeare's sonnets, but there aren't any on the shelves. Have some come in?"

"I'm afraid not," he said, staring at her. "But I have a copy you can borrow, if you'd like."

Elizabeth felt his eyes moving all over her. She crossed her arms in front of her and uncomfortably shifted her weight from one foot to the other. "That's all right—I don't want to bother you."

"Not at all. It would be my pleasure. I'll be right back," he said as he wheeled himself down the hallway.

He returned a few minutes later with the book. "I hope you enjoy it."

"Thank you," she said, taking the book from him. "I really appreciate it."

He looked deeply into her eyes. "Anytime, Elizabeth. Anytime."

Elizabeth shuddered. *How does he know my name?* she wondered as she headed back to her study table. *There has to be a reasonable explanation,* she told herself to calm the anxiety she felt. Maybe he heard Maia or someone else saying her name. Still, there was something unnerving about the way he looked at her, something that sent a cold chill down Elizabeth's spine. *Get a grip,* Elizabeth ordered herself. *Don't overreact.*

"Any luck with the library guy?" Maia asked as she plopped down in the chair next to Elizabeth.

She pointed to the book. "He lent us his very own copy."

"That was pretty nice," Maia said, looking impressed.

Elizabeth nodded, biting her lip. "Maia, I wanted to ask you about something," she said cautiously, unsure how Maia would react. "I'm organizing an empowerment rally for women who have been victims of crime, and I was wondering if you'd be willing to help me."

Maia was looking nervous, so Elizabeth continued before she had a chance to say no. "This is something they've been doing at campuses all over the country. It's called 'Take Back the Night.' It would give you a chance to be with people who've had similar experiences."

"When is it?" Maia asked cautiously.

"The day after tomorrow." She saw the look of alarm on Maia's face. "I know, that isn't much time—but we don't have a lot of time." Elizabeth had a feeling that Maia knew what she meant, without her having to explain it. "That's why I need your help. I need you to tell as many people as possible so that we can have a good crowd."

"Sure, I'll tell people," Maia answered. She opened her notebook.

"I hope you'll come, Maia," Elizabeth said gently. "I think it's going to be a pretty incredible experience."

Maia sat still, obviously deep in thought. Elizabeth casually opened the Shakespeare book so Maia wouldn't feel pressured for an immediate answer. The book was worn, and several pages had been torn out.

"I don't know, Liz," Maia began softly. "I don't want anyone to know what I went through."

"You don't have to give me an answer right away. Just keep it in mind."

"I think it's a really good idea and everything, but I don't want to be there," Maia continued hastily. "Why don't I help you organize it instead? You know—make posters and stuff."

Elizabeth sighed. "Sure, Maia. Anything you want." She started putting her books into her backpack. "I just hope my powers of persuasion are more effective when I talk to Jessica."

It had been hours since the sun had set, and Bruce watched the last few embers of the fire die out. It was too dark to gather more wood—they'd get lost in the endless forest. Bruce had thought of burning some of their clothes, but they couldn't sacrifice that protection from the cold. The temperature had dropped a lot in the last few hours; it was going to be a rough night.

Bruce couldn't see Lila in the darkness, but he could feel her next to him. Her arms were wrapped tightly around him and her head was against his chest. Every few minutes they rubbed each other's hands to keep them warm.

Lila's teeth were chattering. Bruce tucked the blanket underneath her to keep out the wind, then held her tight. But it didn't seem to work—she continued to shiver.

"Are you all right?" he asked, trying to keep the worry out of his voice.

"Yes . . ." Lila said sleepily.

Bruce pressed his body close to hers. There had to be something he could do to keep her warm. The biggest danger facing both of them was hypothermia. He was still alert, but Lila seemed to be drifting off to sleep.

Keep her awake, he thought. Bruce's senses were suddenly alive, heightened by the panic that was setting in. His heart started to pound. He felt warm blood coursing through his veins.

"Stay awake, Lila," he said firmly.

"Hmmmm . . ." she answered. She was still shivering.

There was no time. He seemed to be losing her. Without thinking, Bruce began unbuttoning his outer shirt. He covered Lila with it, ignoring the freezing wind that ripped through his torso.

Isabella walked around the camping supply store in a daze. There were aisles and aisles of lanterns, fishing rods, camp stoves—even freeze-dried food. In another section of the store were rock-climbing equipment, mountain bikes, frame packs for hiking. She felt completely lost. All she wanted were a few simple things to take Danny out on an overnight camping trip for their anniversary. But she had no idea where to begin.

She wandered over to the tent display. *Now we're getting somewhere,* she thought. They'd definitely need a tent. But which one? There were at least ten on the display floor.

In the corner was a small blue tent that looked just about the right size for the two of them.

"I might as well try it out," Isabella said to herself as she slipped off her heels and crawled into the tent. She zipped the door closed to get the full effect.

She lay down in the tent, and the hard floor hurt her back. She stretched out her legs as much as she could and imagined what it would be like to spend the night in here. Isabella closed her eyes and tried to relax, but it was impossible. She felt like she was in a coffin.

I think I've had enough, Isabella said to herself as she sat up, hitting her head on the canvas. Maybe camping wasn't such a great idea after all—there were tons of other great presents she could give him for their anniversary. *Why is Danny so crazy about camping, anyway?* As far as Isabella could tell, she wasn't missing anything. She pulled on the zipper, anxious to get back onto the display floor.

The zipper wouldn't budge. Isabella yanked again. She could see that part of the canvas was jammed into the zipper, but she couldn't fix it. *Stay calm,* she told herself. The walls felt as if they were closing in on her.

Isabella tugged again. "Open!" she shouted. Isabella got to her feet and with her body crouched down, she pulled on the zipper with all her strength. The zipper broke free and Isabella heard a loud *rip* as the tent opened.

"Do you need any help, ma'am?" the salesman asked.

"Uh, yes," Isabella said as she looked at him through the gaping hole she'd made. "I'd like to buy this tent."

*   *   *

A thin line of soft yellow light appeared across the horizon. It was still quite dark, but Lila could make out the silhouettes of the trees and the edge of the ravine. She could also see the faint outline of Bruce's profile.

"We made it through another night," she said as she watched the dawn. With the warmth of the sun, they could get through the next few hours. It wasn't a lot of time, but Lila was grateful for every moment.

"Maybe I can gather some wood later on. Then we can search the ravine for some rocks or something to start another fire," Bruce said.

Lila didn't have the energy to gather wood, and she doubted Bruce really did either. They had spent the entire night talking. They had told each other the most intimate, personal details of their lives. Lila had told Bruce things she never told anyone—not even Tisiano.

Lila nestled against his chest, and Bruce rested his chin on top of her head. It felt good to be in his arms. Together they had made it this far. Maybe they could make it farther.

The morning light was slightly stronger now, and Lila looked up to see Bruce's face. He was staring down at her. His gaze had an intensity that reminded her of the glowing embers from the night before. She felt the rise and fall of his chest as his breathing became heavier.

Their eyes were still locked as Bruce's head bent down and Lila reached up to meet him. She closed her eyes only when she felt the soft warmth of his lips touching hers.

Suddenly there was a roaring in Lila's ears, and she could feel the blood rushing through her veins. She ran her fingers through Bruce's thick hair, kissing him with an energy she didn't know she had. All the frustration, loneliness, and fear that had built up inside both of them had ignited into an explosive embrace.

Bruce's lips traced the line of Lila's jaw, then moved down her neck. The roaring in her ears grew louder. Lila no longer felt the stinging cold; she was only aware of the heat of Bruce's breath on her skin. In that instant, nothing else seemed to matter. It was as if they were the last two people left on earth.

Chapter Eight

The roaring in Lila's ears became so loud that she finally opened her eyes. In the distance she saw a black oval on the horizon.

"Bruce, look!" she shouted.

Bruce looked up at the helicopter that was moving toward them.

"I can't believe it," Lila said, choked with tears. "We're going to be rescued!"

Bruce hugged her excitedly. "We did it, Li! We made it!"

As Lila watched the helicopter she suddenly felt lighter, energized.

Bruce ripped his shirt in half and began waving the pieces in the air so that the helicopter could see them. It slowed as it approached, then hovered above the spot where Bruce and Lila were standing. A rescue ladder was dropped at their feet.

"We are unable to land in this area . . ." the voice

over the loudspeaker boomed. ". . . You'll have to use the ladder."

Lila clutched Bruce's arm. The excitement of finally going home was mixed with fear. More than anything, she wanted to be in the helicopter, on her way home. But the thought of being suspended fifty feet in the air on a flimsy rope ladder made her completely nauseous. "I can't do it, Bruce. I just can't."

"We have to, Lila! There's no other way!" Bruce shouted above the noise of the helicopter.

Lila tried to take a step toward the ladder, but she froze. "I can't."

Bruce led her to the ladder, placing her hands firmly on one of the lower rungs. "Go ahead," he said bravely. "I'll be right behind you. Nothing's going to happen."

Lila stepped on the first rung. The ladder began to move back and forth. Her terror-filled eyes looked behind her to find Bruce. His arms reached out to the ropes on either side of her to steady the ladder.

She continued slowly upward. The spiraling wind created by the chopper whipped her long hair wildly, blocking her vision when she looked up. She felt her way carefully up the ladder, clenching her fingers tightly around the rope.

When she was nearly halfway to the top, Bruce started to climb. The ladder swung out of control. Lila stopped where she was and looked at the ground far below. A spotlight shone brightly down on them, making Lila feel as if she were in a circus, performing some acrobatic feat. If only she had a safety net.

"You're doing great, Li!" Bruce called to her breathlessly. He had nearly caught up to her.

Lila looked down. The ladder swung perilously over the ravine—its jagged edges were waiting below. The view made her sick to her stomach, and Lila felt her knees begin to give way.

"Don't give up on me now," Bruce urged. He was directly behind her, helping Lila steady herself. "Take it one step at a time."

She climbed higher, letting Bruce guide her toward the helicopter. She felt sheltered in his arms. Safe.

Seconds later, two men reached down from above. Their strong arms pulled her to safety.

"Is everything ready for the march?" Nina asked Elizabeth as they waited for the class before theirs to leave the auditorium.

"Yeah, pretty much. Everything seems to be in place," Elizabeth answered. "I think this is going to be quite a rally. You'll be there, won't you?"

Nina nodded vigorously. "I wouldn't miss it. And I'm going to a Black Student Union meeting tonight, so I'll try to get some people to go."

"Then maybe all of you could stop by and try to convince my sister to go along with you," Elizabeth said glumly.

"Jessica still doesn't want to go?"

Elizabeth shook her head. "I don't know. She

definitely isn't beating the door down to join. But you know Jess—she always makes her decisions at the last minute." The door to the auditorium opened and a few students trickled out. Elizabeth stepped aside to let them by.

"I'm sure she's nervous about it, but she'll come around," Nina said.

Celine Boudreaux walked out the door, wearing a leopard-print halter and a black velvet mini. She squeezed past Elizabeth and Nina, her honey-blond curls bouncing as she walked.

"I don't think I've ever seen her go to class," Nina whispered.

"That was Professor Owen's class. She makes a habit of going."

"Celine likes history?" Nina asked with surprise.

Elizabeth laughed. "Hardly! I think she just goes for the scenery."

A moment later Professor Owen came out of the auditorium with several female students in tow. He was young, with dark hair and a boyish grin. No matter how hard he tried to separate himself from his admirers, they continued to follow him.

"Now I understand." Nina laughed. They walked into the room and took their usual seats in the third row, center. "So, has Celine been harassing you lately?" Nina asked. She dropped her backpack onto an empty seat. "Any more strangled roses or tortured Barbie dolls?"

"No, not exactly." Elizabeth had almost forgotten

106

about the scarf that had been taken from her in the library, only to be found later tied in a noose, holding a white rose. Nina had found another noose near Elizabeth's books, but that time there had been a Barbie doll in it. Nina swore that she caught a glimpse of Celine running away from the scene. It hadn't occurred to Elizabeth before, but suddenly she wondered—had Celine been behind the latest round of notes?

"What do you mean by *not exactly?*"

Elizabeth took her notebook and a pen from her backpack. "I've gotten some strange notes lately, but I don't know if Celine is involved. To tell you the truth, I haven't given them that much thought. I've been distracted."

Nina stared at her, an expression of horror on her face. "Elizabeth, you can't ignore this."

Elizabeth opened her book. "I don't think it's that big a deal, Nina. It's strange, but I'm not going to flip out about it."

Nina shook her head. "It is a big deal. You may not think it's serious now, but it could get a lot worse."

Elizabeth was slightly unnerved by Nina's serious reaction. Seeing how upset she was, Elizabeth had to wonder if maybe she wasn't taking the whole thing seriously enough. "Are you sure this isn't just a harmless prank?" Elizabeth asked.

"No way," Nina said adamantly. "Something weird is definitely going on. And you'd better figure out who's responsible—before it's too late."

*   *   *

The helicopter propellers thundered as Bruce and Lila were lifted out of the mountain valley. Lila's knees were still shaking, and tears of relief were streaming down her face. She stared out the window until the snow-capped peaks disappeared from sight. They were on their way home.

One of the medics covered Bruce and Lila with a thick blanket. They were given cups of hot coffee. Lila sipped the coffee, enjoying the warmth of the hot liquid trickling down her throat.

"We radioed the hospital that you're coming. They'll notify your families," the medic said.

Lila looked up to find Bruce smiling at her. Even though she was excited and happy to be going home, Lila was filled with longing. She could still taste Bruce's kiss and feel the warmth of his embrace. She wished they could just pick up where they left off. As if reading her mind, Bruce put his arm around her shoulders and drew her close to him.

Lila closed her eyes and pictured what it would be like when they returned to Sweet Valley. Who would be waiting for them? she wondered. Her family would definitely be there. What about their friends? Lila imagined how much fun it would be to call them up, one by one, and tell them about the ordeal she'd been through. "You'll never guess what happened," she'd begin. "Bruce and I were in a plane crash . . ."

"Look," Bruce said, pointing out the window. "We're almost home."

Lila saw the foamy waves of the ocean and the sandy beaches below. The houses were neat little squares on tree-lined streets, and the traffic was getting heavy as people rushed off to work. Lila had traveled all over the world, but as far as she was concerned, this was the best view ever.

Lila reached out and squeezed Bruce's hand as they descended. She held her breath as the helicopter dropped lower and lower. It wasn't until the helicopter had actually touched the landing pad that she exhaled. She wanted to run outside and kiss the ground.

Bruce and Lila were escorted out of the helicopter. Two ambulances were waiting for them and several paramedics stood by. The warm air hit them like a blast from a furnace. People swarmed around them.

"Ma'am, please lie down," a short, bald man requested as he eased Lila onto the stretcher. She was immediately covered with wool blankets and straps were fastened to keep her from moving.

Bruce stood over her, gazing wordlessly into her eyes. *Don't leave me.* The words kept turning over and over in her mind. Bruce gently stroked her cheek and forehead, traced the outline of her lips with his fingertips. Then he lowered his face toward hers, and their lips met in a slow kiss.

The ambulance doors were thrown open and Lila was moved into the back. She strained to watch as Bruce was being strapped onto a stretcher. An indescribable sense of loss hit her as she realized he was being loaded into the other ambulance. They'd been separated.

The doors slammed shut. Paramedics scurried around her, covering her face with an oxygen mask, checking her blood pressure, bandaging her wounds. Lila felt her body relax completely, as if she were floating. It was only a matter of seconds before she was overtaken by the sweet tranquility of sleep.

"Are you sure you're feeling all right, Steven?" Jessica asked as she dug her toes deep into the sand. The warmth of the sun felt good on her skin. Jessica breathed a sigh of contentment as the ocean breeze gently blew her long blond hair. "Hey, Billie!" Jessica shouted. "When did your boyfriend get to be so nice?"

Billie laughed as she ran for the Frisbee that Elizabeth had thrown over her head. "I don't know," she called. "This is the first I've seen of it."

Steven frowned. "Since when is it such a big deal that a guy treats three lovely ladies to lunch and an afternoon at the beach?"

"Since that guy was you," Jessica chided. She raised her arms to protect herself from the handful of sand Steven threw in her direction. "I'm just kidding!"

Billie tossed the Frisbee. It was picked up by a gust of wind, and instead of heading toward Elizabeth, it was thrown into a wave. "So, what's on your mind, Steven?" Jessica asked as she watched her twin wade through the ocean water to retrieve the Frisbee.

"What do you mean?" he asked innocently.

"You know what I'm talking about," Jessica said, her eyes perfectly reflecting the blue of the ocean waves. "You want to talk to me about something. Don't deny it," she said as he opened his mouth to protest. "The pizza, the long drive to the beach—you're doing exactly what Dad does when he wants to talk to us about something."

Steven blushed. "Am I really acting like Dad?"

Jessica nodded. "Out with it."

Steven grabbed a stick and began to draw in the sand. "Since you figured me out, I might as well come clean. I wanted to talk to you about James."

The warmth of the sun seemed to disappear, leaving Jessica feeling only the chill of the ocean breeze. Her eyes were clouded, like the Pacific after a storm. "Please—I'm not in the mood for a lecture. . . ."

"I'm not going to lecture you," Steven said. "I just wanted to know how you're handling everything."

Jessica felt awkward. How could she discuss something like this with her brother? "I'm OK, I guess."

"You know, Jess, you can talk to me anytime. I'm here for you." The Frisbee landed at Steven's feet and he threw it back to Billie. "So is Elizabeth. I know you have a lot to deal with now, so you might not even realize it, but your sister's gone to a lot of trouble to help you through this."

"Steven, please get to the point," Jessica answered. She appreciated her brother's concern, but she was sick of talking about James.

Steven drew a triangle in the sand. "I think you should go to the march."

Jessica stared out into the foamy waves. Now she was getting it from Steven. It seemed as though everyone was putting pressure on her. They all wanted to take control of her life, but Jessica was determined to keep any little bit of it she still had. "We'll see. I might—I might not," she said flatly.

"After all the organizing she's done, the least you can do is show up."

"It's not that easy," Jessica answered. "I'm having a hard time. I'd like to say yes, but I never know how I'm going to feel one moment to the next, let alone a day from now. Would you rather have me lie to you and say that I'll be there, then never show up?"

Steven sighed. "I just think it's something you need right now. And if you won't do it for yourself, at least do it for Liz."

Jessica covered her legs with cool sand. "Steven, you didn't tell Mike about any of this, did you?"

Steven's brow furrowed. "No—did you want me to?"

"I don't know," Jessica answered. Mike had always been so protective of her when they were married. She imagined how nice it would be to have him worried about her again. At the same time, it scared her to think of how angry Mike would get if he found out that someone had hurt her.

"You may not have much choice, anyhow," Steven said. "You know Mike—he has his own

112

sources." Billie and Elizabeth ran past the two of them. "Hey, where are you going?" Steven asked.

"To get some ice cream," Billie called.

"Wait for us!" Steven answered, getting to his feet. "Jess, please don't forget what we talked about. Give it some thought. And remember, I'm a law student, so if you decide you want to take this further—"

"Thanks, big brother. I appreciate it," Jessica cut in before he finished. "I'll let you know if I need any help." Steven didn't look convinced. "I promise!"

"OK, everybody, listen up!" Magda shouted to the group of Thetas and Sigmas that had gathered on the quad for a late-afternoon meeting. "We're here to find out all we can about the disappearance of Bruce and Lila. I've divided you up into pairs. Those of you with cars will go to the surrounding towns, and the rest will stay here on campus."

Jessica stared down at the ground she was sitting on, nervously pulling up tufts of grass. The calm and peace she had felt at the beach earlier in the day had melted away at the sight of Mariela and James together. They were only a few feet away from where Jessica was sitting. When Mariela caught Jessica glancing in their direction, she grabbed James's hand.

"Is everything clear?" Magda asked the crowd. "If you have any questions, you can ask me after I announce the teams." She pushed up the sleeves of her sweatshirt and flipped through the pages on her clipboard. "Peter?" she called.

"Yes, ma'am," he answered.

"Since you have a car, we'd like you to go into town. You'll be working with Alison."

Alison batted her eyelashes in Peter's direction. "Have you ever gone cruising in a Jaguar convertible?" he asked her.

Alison pouted her lips demurely. "Only once," she answered. She picked up their posters, and they headed for the parking lot. Magda made a check mark on her list. "James Montgomery? There you are," she said as she located him. "You and Mariela will be going off campus."

Jessica held back the urge to jump up and hold Mariela back. It scared her to think of James being alone with anyone, especially one of her sorority sisters. The couple got up and walked toward the parking lot—Mariela's arm protectively entwined in his. James didn't even look in her direction. *There's nothing you can do,* Jessica thought, trying to calm herself. *She doesn't believe you anyway.*

Jessica and Isabella were assigned to work together around campus. They picked up a stack of posters and started stapling them to bulletin boards. Jessica worked without saying a word.

"Don't let them get you down," Isabella said as they were hanging a poster outside the cafeteria.

"Who?" Jessica asked, making sure the poster was straight.

Isabella looked around. "You know," she whispered. "James and Mariela. She just enjoys rubbing your nose in it."

Jessica secured the poster. She wondered where James and Mariela were now, and if James had tried anything with her. She'd never be able to forgive herself if Mariela was hurt.

"Iz, I need to talk to you," Jessica said, trying not to cry.

"What is it?" Isabella looked alarmed. They sat down on a bench.

Jessica told Isabella the entire story about her date with James and what had happened to Maia. Isabella listened quietly, her eyes wide with disbelief.

"I had no idea that was why you broke up," Isabella said when Jessica had finished. "I thought you two just had a fight or something."

Jessica dried her tears. "That's what most people think. It's not the kind of thing you advertise."

"And now Mariela is seeing him," Isabella said seriously. "What are you going to do?"

Jessica shrugged. "I tried to warn her, but she didn't listen. I couldn't bring myself to tell her the whole story. What else can I do?"

"I don't know," Isabella said. "You don't want to press charges?"

"No. I don't want to go through that."

"But you do want to warn people about him, right?" Isabella asked.

"Yes . . ." Jessica wondered what she was getting at.

Isabella seemed lost in thought. "Are you planning to go to the Take Back the Night rally?"

"I don't know." Jessica studied her quizzically. "You're losing me."

Isabella stared at Jessica. "I think I know how you can get the word out about James without pressing charges—but you need to go to the march tomorrow night," she said, her warm gray eyes sparkling.

Jessica's stomach was tied up in knots. Steven was right—Elizabeth had gone to a lot of trouble for her. Jessica didn't want to disappoint her sister. At the same time, it frightened her to think of all the people she'd be facing at the rally—people who might find out what had happened to her. Then she remembered Mariela, clutching onto James. As it was, James was free to strike again—and if he did, Jessica would never be able to forgive herself.

"Can you trust me?" Isabella asked.

Jessica swallowed hard. "It's the only choice I've got," she answered.

Chapter
Nine

Elizabeth stood on the steps of the library, passing out candles and setting up microphones for the rally. It was supposed to start in twenty minutes, and already there was a huge crowd. Nina had run back to the store three times already, because they kept running out of candles.

Elizabeth handed out the last candle in the box. "We'll have more any minute now," she said to the crowd. *I hope Nina gets back soon,* Elizabeth thought.

"Can you believe the crowd?" Tom said as he attached the WSVU microphone to the podium. Elizabeth shook her head. There were so many more people than she'd dared hope would turn out.

Elizabeth scanned the crowd. It was dusk, and she had trouble seeing. Among the sea of faces and posters, she sought a glimpse of either Maia or Jessica. So far, neither one had shown up.

"I'm back!" Nina shouted, carrying a huge box

of candles. "This is it—the store manager said we cleaned him out!"

"I guess this will have to do," Elizabeth said gratefully.

"Liz, can you stand at the podium? I need to set up the camera," Tom called.

"I'll be right there!" Elizabeth shouted.

"Elizabeth—we're going to need a sound check as soon as you're ready," one of the technicians called.

Elizabeth felt as though she was being pulled in a hundred directions at once. "Can you pass out the candles for me, Nina?"

"Sure thing," Nina said, moving the box over to where the line was.

Elizabeth stood behind the podium. "Is this good?" she asked Tom.

"Great. Now give me a big smile."

Elizabeth stuck out her tongue at him.

"Beautiful." Tom winked at her. "Now sit tight while I adjust the tripod."

Elizabeth tapped the microphone with her fingernail. "Testing, one, two, three. Testing." The technician adjusted the levels and nodded at Elizabeth to try again. "Testing. Can everyone hear me back there?" she asked. The crowd roared.

"The effect you have on these people!" Tom said as he made the final adjustments.

"What can I say?" Elizabeth laughed. She was stunned by the enthusiasm and energy of the crowd.

Apparently the women of SVU were more interested in Take Back the Night issues than Elizabeth had ever imagined.

Elizabeth watched people go by, hoping to spot Jessica. Now that the event was about to begin, Elizabeth was more sure than ever that this rally was exactly what Jessica needed. Elizabeth hated to think that Jessica might miss it.

Elizabeth scanned the crowd one last time. *Where are you, Jessica?* she wondered.

Isabella knocked lightly on the door and walked into Jessica's room. "Are you ready?" she asked.

"I think so." Jessica brushed her hair and checked her makeup. "How do I look?" she asked.

"Like a girl who's going to be late if you don't hurry up," Isabella joked. "I could hear them chanting from Theta House."

Jessica looked at her with surprise. "There are that many people at the rally?" She tucked her white blouse tightly into the waistband of her jeans.

Isabella nodded. "Tons. But that's good. You'll blend in with the crowd. It'll warm you up for later."

"I don't know about this," Jessica said, nervously checking her hair in the mirror.

Isabella straightened the collar of Jessica's blouse. "If you ever feel your confidence waning, just think about James. Remember why you're doing this," she said. "Did you write down what you're going to say?"

"A little." Jessica's hands were starting to shake.

"I'm sure my mind will blank out when the time comes," she said. "So when are we going to do it?"

"You just go along with the march, and I'll catch up to Tom. I'll try to set something up for immediately after the rally." Isabella grabbed Jessica's arm. "Come on, let's go."

Jessica's stomach was aching as they headed toward the quad. When she heard the chanting, Jessica tried to turn back, but Isabella held her firmly by the arm. *Why am I doing this?* she wondered. *Why?*

The girls reached the edge of the crowd just as Elizabeth stepped onto the platform. Hundreds of students had come. They were yelling and clapping, chanting. Jessica stood there, taking it all in, as she waited for Elizabeth to speak.

"Thank you all for coming," Elizabeth said when the crowd quieted down.

Then Elizabeth began the speech that Jessica knew she'd been preparing for the past two days. "We're here tonight to take a stand. We're here to protest the crimes that have been committed against us as women. We are here—as victims of rape, sexual harassment, discrimination, domestic violence—to say that we refuse to tolerate this kind of treatment."

Jessica and Isabella moved closer to the library steps for a better view of the podium. Elizabeth's words had captivated the audience. Jessica smiled and gave her twin a mental pat on the back—even though she was standing in front of hundreds of people, Elizabeth was as poised as she always was.

". . . We are here tonight to reclaim what is ours. We're taking control of our minds and our bodies. . . ."

The crowd roared. Jessica looked at the people jumping around and waving their posters. Her heart was pounding.

". . . Tonight, as women, we demand the same respect that everyone deserves. . . ."

Jessica was swept up in the energy around her. She started clapping and cheering with the rest of the women. Jessica looked around at the people in the crowd. She recognized a lot more of the group than she'd expected. Jessica smiled at everyone she knew. *Maybe there's more support out there than I realized,* she thought.

Elizabeth lit a candle and held it high in the air. "Women, unite! Take back the night!" The marchers quieted as Elizabeth left the podium and went down into the crowd. She lit someone's candle in the front row, and that person passed on the flame. One by one, they lit the candles. The chanting had started out quietly, with only a few voices, but as the flame spread throughout the crowd the words "Women Unite, Take Back the Night" rang out clearly into the night.

"How did the date go, Enid?" T-Squared asked.

"Pretty well," Alex answered. She'd been incredibly excited to tell T-Squared about Noah, but now as she talked to him, all the enthusiasm seemed to drain out of her body. Suddenly she was focused only on the voice over the phone. Her feelings for Noah faded into the background.

The voice at the other end of the phone was calm and soothing. "Tell me all about it," he coaxed.

Alex turned down the sound on her television set. "I don't want to bore you with the details—but I had a great time."

"Are you going to go out again?" T-Squared asked.

"Oh, I don't know," she replied vaguely. It was the truth—she didn't know for sure. And she couldn't think of a good reason to tell T-Squared that she was pretty confident she and Noah would be seeing each other again. It was almost as if she wanted T-Squared to think she was unattached.

"Even if you never see the guy again, at least you had the opportunity to find out for yourself whether or not you were interested. You never know how something will turn out until you give it a try." For a moment, Alex thought T-Squared sounded very optimistic, almost *glad* that she might not be seeing Noah again.

I wonder what he looks like, Alex thought. Suddenly she had an overwhelming desire to find out. She stared vacantly at the TV screen. On WSVU students were marching and chanting. Alex clicked off the set. It was time to take the plunge.

"I was thinking," Alex began slowly. "We've been

talking on the phone so much—I feel like I've known you for a long time."

"Same here, Enid," he answered.

So far, so good, she thought. Alex crossed her fingers for good luck. "It's funny, though, how we've never even met. Would you like to get together with me sometime?"

The pause at the other end of the line seemed to last an eternity. Alex was almost certain that T-Squared could hear the sound of her heart pounding through the receiver. Finally he answered, "I don't think that would be such a good—"

Alex hung up before she could hear the rest. Why had she done that? Why? She should have known that T-Squared wouldn't want to meet a girl who always called a hot line to unload her problems on a virtual stranger. And now there was no way she could ever call again. She was too embarrassed. *Way to go, Alex,* she said to herself. *You sure know how to ruin everything.*

"Women unite! Take back the night!" the crowd continued to chant as they marched across campus. Students were coming out of their dorms, waiting outside to watch the group pass by. Some people ran out to join them.

Jessica was chanting at the top of her lungs, raising her fist high in the air. Her body felt light, like an enormous burden had been lifted from her shoulders. She was back in control of her life.

Jessica made her way to the front of the crowd

where her sister was marching and put her arm around her. Elizabeth turned.

"You came!" Elizabeth shouted, hugging Jessica. "I'm so glad."

"Me too!" Jessica shouted above the noise of the crowd. "Thanks for everything." Elizabeth gave her a squeeze.

Isabella ran up to Jessica. "Tom says he can do it now if you're ready."

"Do what?" Elizabeth looked puzzled.

Jessica took her by the hand and pulled her aside. "I'm going on WSVU."

Elizabeth stared at Jessica in shock. "What are you talking about?" Instead of answering, Jessica jogged over to the camera crew.

"Thanks for doing this, Jess. You're going to be great," Tom said encouragingly. "Why don't you turn around so we can get a shot of the marchers behind you?"

Jessica turned around. She glanced over at Isabella. "How do I look?"

Isabella smoothed down a few hairs that were out of place. "Fabulous. Do you remember what you want to say?"

"I don't know." Jessica smiled nervously. "I guess I'll have to wing it."

"Will someone please tell me what's going on?" Elizabeth said, appealing to Tom for help.

"No time now, honey," he said. "We're on in thirty seconds."

                    *   *   *

Maia watched the march from the window of her dorm room. She had heard the marchers chanting as they passed outside, and for a moment she considered joining them. Instead she stood silently, taking in the sights and sounds of the demonstration.

Maybe I should have gone, Maia thought as she sat in the solitude of her room. She would have loved to have been part of all the excitement. But she couldn't help but think of the other people—the ones who were watching the event on TV or standing by on the sidelines. Those were the people she was afraid of. She didn't want anyone seeing her as a victim or, even worse, as a hysterical female trying to get attention.

Maia watched as WSVU returned from their commercial break. Standing in front of the camera were Tom Watts and Jessica Wakefield.

"Jessica?" Maia said aloud as she stared at the screen. She had wondered if Jessica had decided to go after all—and there she was, right on TV, looking great.

"We're back—with coverage of the Take Back the Night march. I'm standing here with Jessica Wakefield, who is one of the participants." Tom turned to Jessica, holding the microphone in front of her.

She is so brave, Maia thought. Why couldn't she do that? Here Maia was, too wimpy to even show up, and Jessica was about to give an interview in front of the entire campus.

". . . Jessica, what do you think of the march so far?" Tom asked her.

"I think it's wonderful. It is going to help raise the awareness of not just the women on this campus, but everyone." Jessica's voice was strong and confident.

"Now I know you have your own reason for coming tonight—do you want to tell us what that is?"

"Yes . . ." The camera pulled in tight, getting a close-up of Jessica's face. "I was sexually assaulted four days ago . . ."

Maia gasped. Was Jessica really going to tell them everything?

". . . by an acquaintance of mine. Actually, we had been dating. He's someone on this campus." Jessica stared directly into the TV camera. "Someone you all know."

Maia threw off the blanket and sat directly in front of the TV set. Her pulse raced. *Tell them, Jessica, tell them who he is.*

"Who did this to you?" Tom asked.

"I can't mention his name," she said loudly. "But he's a star athlete who plays on both the soccer and the football teams. He's a premed student and the treasurer of the Sigmas. I think everyone knows who I'm talking about. . . ."

Maia's heart leapt into her throat. There was only one person who matched that description.

"Why are you bringing this up tonight?" Tom asked.

"Because this person doesn't seem to realize the damage he's done. I want to be sure that he isn't able to do this to anyone else." The camera pulled back again, showing the dozens and dozens of women standing behind Jessica.

"Is there anything else you'd like to add?"

"Yes." Jessica smiled. "I want to say thank you to my sister Elizabeth for organizing this march. It was great."

"Damn!" Noah slammed down the receiver in frustration. *Why didn't she give me a chance to explain?* He wanted to meet Enid more than anything, and he wanted her to know it. Only the rules of the hot line held him back.

Is Enid really Alex? Noah wondered. He glanced at the caller ID box on the corner of the desk. It was the one thing that held the answer to the mystery.

Using the box for anything other than emergencies was not only breaking a major rule, it was unethical as well. It went completely against Noah's beliefs in caller privacy. Yet he felt himself magnetically drawn to the small instrument. There was no other way. He'd have to use it.

Unfortunately the box could only identify a caller if they were on the line. He'd have to wait until Enid called back—*if* she ever called back. Noah vowed that if she did, he'd find out the truth. He couldn't let her slip through his fingers again.

"I'm so proud of you," Elizabeth said, hugging her sister warmly. "You did a very brave thing tonight."

Jessica smiled. "I'm glad I came. This was a wonderful idea."

They walked back to Dickenson Hall arm in arm. Except for a few students heading to the library for some late-night studying, the quad was bare. Despite the peacefulness of the night, Elizabeth had the strange sensation that someone was following them back to the dorm. She turned around quickly, but no one was in sight.

"So, how do you feel now that you made that announcement on WSVU?" Elizabeth asked, the anxiety subsiding. *You're imagining things again, Elizabeth,* she told herself. *You're just too stressed out.*

"Actually, I feel a lot better—like I can do anything." Jessica smiled. "And I've made a decision," she announced.

"What's that?" The lampposts were casting an eerie shadow onto the walkway. She walked faster as they neared the building.

"Are we running a marathon or what?" Jessica asked.

Elizabeth kept up the pace. "It's chilly out here," she said hastily. "So what did you decide?"

"I'm going to press charges," Jessica answered seriously.

"Oh, Jessica, I'm so glad!" Elizabeth hugged her twin. "That's great news." She quickly unlocked the door to the building.

Jessica walked into the dorm, and Elizabeth followed on her heels. She turned to close the door firmly behind her. Although she couldn't see anyone in the darkness, Elizabeth felt sure that a pair of eyes was out there somewhere, watching her.

"What's this?" Jessica said when they reached the room.

Elizabeth gasped. On the floor in front of the door was a small white envelope. Jessica picked it up before Elizabeth could stop her.

Jessica read the note aloud. "For Jessica. Carry this with you—use it whenever you need help." Inside the envelope was a silver whistle.

Chapter
Ten

Magda and Denise sat cross-legged on the parlor floor of Theta House. Jessica was telling them about James, but they already seemed to know most of the details. She was amazed at how quickly the news had spread.

"Why didn't you tell us, Jess?" Magda asked. "You know we would have been there for you."

Jessica hugged a brocade pillow. "I know. It's just that I couldn't tell anyone—I was ashamed. I didn't think anyone would believe me."

Alison and Mariela walked in, grinding the conversation to a halt. Mariela threw her books on the floor and took a seat in a chair. Alison sat on the couch and crossed her legs demurely. Despite the cool elegance of her posture, Alison's dull slate eyes seemed to be smoldering. "What brings you here, Jessica?" she said sourly.

It was obvious that they were ready for a showdown. Alison had tried to oust Jessica from the sorority on numerous occasions but had failed. She still loved to be a thorn in Jessica's side whenever possible.

"I'm just having a conversation with my friends," Jessica answered evenly. She always tried to let Alison's digs roll right off her.

"Would that conversation involve a certain star athlete you dated at one time?" Alison said snidely.

"If you mean James, yes. We were talking about him." Jessica turned her attention back to Magda and Denise.

"And I'm sure it was all good," Alison sneered.

Jessica could see that it was no use trying to avoid a confrontation. Alison and Mariela had sunk in their claws, struggling to engage her in a fight. "What are you getting at, Alison? Whatever's on your mind, I wish you'd just say it." Jessica's voice held a cold edge.

"How could you embarrass me like this?" Mariela interjected. Her face was red. "What did I do to you?"

"I didn't do this to hurt you," Jessica answered truthfully. "James is dangerous. You wouldn't listen to me."

Mariela glared at her. "I can't believe that you're so jealous that you'd stoop to this. What's wrong with you?"

"I don't know why you're pulling this little stunt," Alison said. "My guess is he rejected you, and you couldn't handle it. But you'd better think twice before you drag James through the mud. He's going to go places someday, and he doesn't need

132

you messing things up. His reputation is a lot more important than your deflated ego." There was a flicker of vengeance in her eyes.

Jessica tried to control the anger rising inside her. Why were they so down on her? She was only trying to stop James from hurting anyone else. "James attacked me, that's all there is to it. I'm not pressing charges to get attention, I just want to make sure he doesn't do this again."

"Come on, guys," Magda said diplomatically. "Why would Jessica put herself through all of this if it weren't true?"

Mariela didn't answer.

Alison swatted the air with her hand, as if she were a queen dismissing a pesky servant. "There could be any number of reasons. All I know is that she doesn't have a case." She glared at Jessica. "I saw you and James at the Sigma party. Everyone saw you. You were all over him. Not to mention the fact that Helen Peterson and Grant Walker saw you at the Mountain Lodge Inn, kicking back a few beers and cuddling in your cozy little booth."

Jessica felt her defenses crumbling. She never realized how many people had seen them together. Alison's point was an exaggerated twisting of the truth, but it was impossible to argue. "Things aren't always what they seem," was all she managed to say.

"Well, it *seems* to me that no one is going to believe your story. After all, who would *you* believe: a suave, sophisticated campus leader and star athlete, or a freshman divorcée with a record?" Alison flashed her a self-satisfied look. "Face it, Jessica Wakefield, you are over on this campus."

"I guess that's everything," Danny said to himself as he loaded the last bag into the library elevator.

Danny closed the elevator door. After much pleading, his boss at the security office had let him borrow a key that gave him special access in the library. Now Danny inserted that key into a special lock on the elevator panel and pushed a red button next to the word *tower*.

While the elevator climbed higher and higher, Danny thought about the night ahead. He'd nearly killed himself with the preparation, but he was finally starting to get excited. The elevator opened, and Danny gasped. The place looked incredible.

Danny walked the perimeter of the room. It was shaped like a huge octagon, and every wall had enormous windows. The room not only had a perfect view of every part of campus but also of miles beyond. Buildings and trees and hills lay below. And in the distance he could see the point where the sparkling ocean met the horizon.

Danny imagined the magnificence of the view at night, and the surprise and wonder on Isabella's face when she saw it. After tonight, Isabella would never accuse him of being unromantic again.

He had borrowed the idea from Tom, then added a few touches of his own. Instead of taking

Isabella to a restaurant, he had ordered takeout. Instead of going to a dance club, he brought his own tape player and collection of jazz tapes. To make sure Isabella would know where to find him, he'd left a rose and a note on her pillow. As soon as she stopped by her room, she'd be on her way.

Danny scurried around the tower room, rushing to get everything done before Isabella arrived. When he was finished, he stood back and gazed at his masterpiece. Everything was perfect. The table was set with a white tablecloth and two red candles. Soft jazz music played in the background. The Chinese food he'd brought was still in paper cartons, keeping warm. It had taken a lot of work, but Danny was certain he'd remembered every last romantic detail. He'd even tucked a tiny slip of paper into Isabella's fortune cookie. It said, *Happy Anniversary, Isabella. Love, Danny.*

Danny straightened his bow tie. "It's show time!" he said aloud. He leaned against a windowpane, hoping the view would calm him down. The only thing left to do was to wait for Isabella. He hoped she would make it soon—the sun was already starting to set. The sky was a soft yellow, streaked with bits of orange-pink, the colors growing deeper with every moment that passed.

Isabella unloaded the last bit of equipment from her Land-Rover. The field behind the library seemed like the perfect spot to set up an overnight camp. It was fairly private, but not too far from civilization.

After she had ripped the tent, Isabella explained her plan to the salesman at the store. He'd seemed to sense that she had never been camping before, so he said he'd get everything together that she'd need.

This seems like an awful lot of stuff for just one night in the pseudo-wilderness, Isabella thought, scratching her head. She had bought a tent, two sleeping bags, a lantern, a stove, a cooler, a frame pack, a tarp, and something that looked like an inflatable raft.

"That must be the air mattress," Isabella said to herself. She had decided that she was entitled to at least one luxury item on this overnight trip—and that was not sleeping on the hard ground.

Isabella looked around and took a deep breath of fresh, clean air. Trees swayed gently in the breeze, and she heard birds chirping all around her. When a squirrel darted past her, Isabella laughed. It was more serene and peaceful than she had ever imagined.

I wonder what Danny's going to think, Isabella thought excitedly. She imagined him walking into his room when he returned from working at the security office. On his desk, she'd left a note giving him directions where to find her.

She didn't have much time. Danny would be returning back from work within the hour. Isabella wanted to set up camp and make dinner before Danny arrived.

Danny's going to be so proud of me, Isabella

thought as she rolled up the sleeves of her flannel shirt and started to blow air into the mattress. Even though camping wasn't her idea of the perfect way to spend their anniversary, she knew Danny would love it.

After several minutes of puffing into the mattress, Isabella started to feel dizzy. *Why isn't this blowing up?* she wondered. She turned the mattress over, and on the underside was a hole; it looked like one of the tent stakes had punctured it. "That's OK; I didn't really need it anyway," Isabella said as she rolled the mattress into a ball and hurled it into the back of the Land-Rover.

What should she do next? *Shelter—that's the most important thing.* Isabella unfolded the tent. Camping wasn't so hard. *All it takes is a little common sense,* Isabella thought proudly. This was going to be a piece of cake.

The first thing she did was sort everything into neat little piles. The canvas in one pile, poles in another, and finally the stakes. Isabella carefully unfolded the instructions. "Before you begin assembly, you will need the following," she read out loud. "Nylon rope, a hammer . . ."

Isabella threw the instructions on the ground and stomped on them with her brand-new hiking boots. Why didn't the salesman tell her that she needed extra tools? Danny would be there any minute—she didn't have time to gather everything she needed.

"Stay cool," she told herself as tears of frustration

began to well up in her eyes. Was everything going to go wrong? "I'll just wait until Danny gets here," she decided resolutely. "Then we'll go get the other things."

In the meantime, there's always dinner. She looked down at the large foil bags lying on the ground. The salesman had convinced her that freeze-dried food was the way to go, so Isabella had decided to try it. She'd picked out one of Danny's favorite meals—chili con carne and ice cream for dessert. *At least dinner will be good,* Isabella thought as she reached for the bags. The food made a strange crunching sound, and Isabella's stomach turned. *Then again, we could always have a pizza delivered.*

Alex sat at her desk, staring at her psychology exam. Right above her name, in bright red, was a *B+*. She'd thought for sure that she'd only pull off a *C* at best. And she had Noah to thank.

Alex tucked the psychology exam into her notebook and began to sort her dirty laundry. She thought back to her study date with Noah, and how wonderful and understanding he was. She felt foolish when she thought about T-Squared and how she'd risked her chances with Noah just to meet someone she had only spoken with on the phone.

She glanced at the phone and felt a pang of guilt. *I should never have hung up on him,* Alex thought. She'd been embarrassed, but T-Squared didn't deserve her behavior. *Maybe I should call him one last time,* she thought. *Just to set things straight.* She dialed the hot line.

"Campus hot line . . ." a female voice answered.

Please let him be there. "Yes—could I please speak with T-Squared?"

"One moment," the voice said.

The time had finally come. Even though she hated the thought of never talking to T-Squared again, it was for the best. She couldn't continue to have these feelings for someone she had never met and ruin her chances with someone so wonderful. As much as it hurt her, she had to say good-bye.

"Noah, just in time," Terry King said as Noah walked through the door of the hot-line office. "There's a call for you on line two."

"Thanks," Noah answered. *Could it be Enid?* he wondered. His stomach fluttered as he dove for the phone. "Hello?" he said into the receiver.

"Hi, T-Squared, this is Enid . . ."

Noah smiled. "Enid, I'm so glad you called."

"I just wanted to apologize for hanging up on you the last time I called. I'm really sorry."

Noah's pulse raced. Finally his chance had come. "No apology necessary," he said, trying not to let his excitement show. "It's not that I didn't want to meet you, but it's a rule. The hot-line operators aren't supposed to get to know the callers personally." Noah looked at the caller ID box. All he had to do was press one little button . . . and he'd know everything.

"I understand," Enid was saying. "I guess I got a little carried away. You've helped me through some very tough times. But now I've made some decisions. I'm starting to get back on track. . . . I guess what I'm trying to say is that I won't need to call the hot line anymore."

Should I really be doing this? Noah wondered as he reached for the box. Terry turned around and looked in Noah's direction. He quickly pulled back his hand. "You won't be calling anymore?" Noah answered.

"No, I think it's for the best."

Please leave, Terry, Noah begged silently. Even though he knew it was a major violation, he had to know if Alex was really the caller. His head ached at the thought of never knowing. "I guess you're right," he said. "But maybe you could call once in a while, just to chat."

"It would probably be better if I didn't. I think I need to learn to be independent, don't you?"

Terry hovered over Noah's desk, shuffling stacks of papers. Noah covered the receiver with his hand. "Can I help you with something?" he hissed at her.

"I'm just looking for an earring I lost," Terry said. "I think it might be around here. . . ." She continued to search the desk.

Noah felt panic starting to rise within him. "I'll look for it," he snapped. He had to get her out of the room before Enid hung up, or he'd never be able to trace the call.

"It was really expensive," Terry insisted.

"Go!" he nearly shouted. "I'll find it." He waved her away.

Terry stared at him strangely, then left the office.

"Hello . . . T-Squared? Are you still there?" Enid said on the other end of the line.

Noah breathed a sigh of relief. "Yes, I'm still here," he answered.

"I almost hung up—I didn't hear anything," Enid said.

I'm so glad you didn't, Noah thought. He pushed the button on the box. Enid's phone number was displayed on the screen. "We had a little crisis here a minute ago," he said with a smile. "But now everything is under control."

"Where is she?" Danny sighed heavily as he sat in the darkness. Isabella was supposed to have been there hours ago. The candles were melting, forming red rivers all over the tablecloth. The batteries in his tape player were dead. Danny opened one of the containers of fried rice to stop his stomach from growling. But the food was cold and unappetizing. It seemed that the only thing that wasn't ruined was the sparkling lights of the city below.

Danny blew out the candles. A thin, gray stream of smoke curled around his head. *Maybe she never went back to her room.* Or maybe she didn't see the note on her pillow. If only he had told her first, instead of trying to make it a surprise. . . .

What a stupid idea, Danny chided himself as he

loosened his tie. *What were you thinking?* He could have kicked himself for planning it this way. Now their whole evening was ruined.

He got up and walked over to the windows. The lights of Sweet Valley glittered in the darkness below. In the tower he felt so removed from it all—as if he were floating on his own magic carpet. Moonbeams were shining through the windows of the tower, casting shadows on the floor. Danny pictured Isabella standing there, with the rays of light illuminating her dark hair and shining in her eyes. They would dance together in the moonlight, with the city at their feet, until the sun came up.

Maybe it's not too late after all, Danny thought. All he had to do was look for her around campus or go to her room and wait for her there. Then they could come back to the tower and enjoy the rest of their anniversary.

Danny put his sports jacket back on and slipped the fortune cookie in his pocket. Then he rushed out the door to the elevator. It didn't matter that dinner had turned into a disaster. They still had a fabulous view of the city. And each other.

Chapter Eleven

"How come you're not eating any of my chocolate cake? You always steal some of my dessert," Tom said.

"I'm not hungry," Elizabeth answered, looking over her shoulder for the tenth time. She scanned the coffeehouse crowd. Everyone seemed absorbed in food and conversation. So why did she feel like she was being stared at?

"OK, Ms. Wakefield." Tom spoke into an invisible microphone. "Would you please tell the good people of Sweet Valley U why you are suddenly acting like you are about to undertake some secret spy mission?" he said in his most journalistic voice.

"No reason," Elizabeth said, trying to seem casual. She spotted Jessica as she walked through the door. Elizabeth waved to her.

"Maybe it's because you've had three cups of coffee," Tom observed. "Too much caffeine always makes *me* paranoid."

"Did I really have that many?" she said with surprise. "I didn't even notice."

"Hi, guys," Jessica said, taking a seat at the table.

Elizabeth could tell immediately that something was wrong. "What is it?" she asked.

"I think I'm going to drop the charges, Liz," Jessica said. She looked upset.

Elizabeth suddenly felt very tired. Everything she had been working for could be tossed out the window. But it wasn't her place to push Jessica into doing something she wasn't comfortable with. "If that's what you want to do . . ."

"I don't know what I want." Jessica shook her head. "I filed the complaint this morning. I felt confident enough to go in front of the committee, but then I made the mistake of going to Theta House."

Elizabeth frowned. She still didn't understand why Jessica wanted to stay in that sorority. They seemed to bring her nothing but trouble.

"What happened?" Tom asked, eating his last bite of cake.

"Alison Quinn happened, that's what. She started telling me that I had no case against James. That I had led him on."

Elizabeth reached out and held her sister's hand. "You know that's not true."

"*I* know it, but Alison was saying that a lot of people saw us together and they think I'm lying. Then Mariela started grilling me too—but I can understand that. She thinks I'm making this all up to get back at

144

James. . . . I couldn't even stand up to them." Jessica's voice cracked. "It's just not worth it."

Elizabeth cringed. What right did they have to treat Jessica that way? It was a shame that a trouble-maker like Alison Quinn could have such a strong influence on Jessica's decision. "Remember what you told me the night of the march?" Elizabeth asked. "You said you didn't want anyone else to go through what you did. Remember?"

Jessica nodded.

"This is going to be tough, but it's important that you stick to it, no matter what Alison or anyone else says. You'll see the disciplinary committee in a few days, and then you can put it all behind you," Elizabeth said.

"We'll be here for you—through all of it," Tom added.

"Thanks," Jessica said. "But it's so hard. When I walk around campus, I feel like everyone is looking at me like I'm some sort of criminal. I don't understand it—I was the one who was attacked, and now I'm being punished for it. It's like James wins twice."

Elizabeth finished her coffee. She had thought that getting Jessica to testify against James was going to be the toughest part of the ordeal. But now she was beginning to realize that the roughest road was still ahead.

Lila dove into her plate of meat loaf, mashed potatoes, and peas with gusto. It wasn't gourmet, but it was probably the most delicious food she had ever tasted. The hospital room she was staying in was small and plain, but to Lila, it was better than the grandest hotels in Europe. Even the crisp, starched sheets felt like imported silk.

Lila smiled to herself. If nothing else, this trauma had made her realize that she took a ton of things for granted. Like the basic necessities of life.

Mrs. Fowler walked into the room. "How's my baby?" she said, giving Lila a kiss on the forehead.

"Fine, Mom," Lila said happily. "Where's Dad?"

"He's talking with Mr. Patman—you know, business." Mrs. Fowler fluffed Lila's pillow.

"I'm going to go see Bruce," Lila said, swinging her legs over to the side of the bed.

Mrs. Fowler rushed over. "No, Lila. You should stay right here." She tucked her back into bed. "Bruce's fine. You'll see him soon."

It won't be soon enough, Lila thought. It felt strange not knowing what he was doing at every moment. She felt lost. It wasn't enough for Lila to know that Bruce was doing fine. She wanted to know how he slept, what he ate, if and when he watched television. She wanted to be part of his life again.

And soon I will be, she thought dreamily. Only another day or so and they'd go back to school. Together.

"Do you need anything?" Mrs. Fowler asked.

"No, thanks," Lila said. *I need Bruce, that's what I need.* Since she couldn't see him, she had to resort to daydreaming. Over the past twenty-four hours, she had imagined their reunion dozens of times. Her favorite scenario was that she'd step out into the hallway and he would be there, waiting for her. Maybe he would be holding a gigantic bouquet of flowers. He'd be so overjoyed to see her that he'd sweep her up in his strong arms and kiss her passionately.

"You rest, dear," Mrs. Fowler said as she sat down. "I'm just going to sit over here and read a magazine."

Lila wrapped herself tightly in her blanket. Was Bruce thinking about her? As much as she tried to suppress them, there were nagging doubts in the back of her mind. What if Bruce changed his mind about the way he felt? What if he didn't care anymore?

Isabella put a lid on what was left of the chili. The salesman had been right—the stuff wasn't half bad. In fact, she had managed to polish off nearly the entire pan while she waited for Danny.

He'll be here any minute, she'd told herself again and again over the last few hours. She had set up camp before sundown, and now it was completely dark, except for the lantern she kept nearby.

She snuggled into her down-filled sleeping bag and opened the bag of freeze-dried ice cream. *What should I do?* she wondered. She had considered going back to his room—just to make sure he hadn't missed the note. But there was a good chance that he was on his way. If he arrived when she'd already left, they'd never connect. It was better to stay right where she was.

This is pretty good, Isabella thought as she bit into the ice cream. It was a strange sensation to be eating something that tasted like ice cream and had the same consistency as ice cream, but wasn't cold. *Danny would get a kick out of this,* she thought. Where was he?

Overall, camping wasn't so bad. In fact, it was kind of fun. Isabella thought she'd never survive without the air mattress or the tent, but she was doing fine. All she needed was a sleeping bag and the stars. She turned off the lantern so she could see them better.

"It's gorgeous!" she said aloud as she looked up at the night sky. It was almost as if she were seeing it for the first time. The stars were like jewels carelessly tossed against a background of royal blue velvet. The moon was rising steadily in the sky, bright and clear. Isabella took another bite of ice cream and wished she had brought a telescope, so she could take a closer look.

The view was spectacular, but Isabella liked the sounds even better. The field was completely still except for the chirping of thousands of crickets and the light breeze that occasionally stirred the trees. *It's like music,* Isabella thought as she slowly drifted off to sleep.

"She looked so beautiful," William White said coolly. "It was incredible to be right next to

Elizabeth and not even have her recognize me."

Celine yawned. "How could she, when you have that dead rat glued to your chin?" she muttered under her breath. William had been carrying on for days about his little meeting with Princess Pea-Brain in the library.

William pulled off his fake beard. "I know she had to turn in the paper yesterday, so she'll be bringing the book back to me soon."

"Willie, honey," Celine purred. "You've worked yourself into a great big tizzy. Why don't you just lie down and relax?"

"You have the note, right?" he continued, as if he hadn't heard her. "You'd better deliver it soon."

"Shhh." Celine pushed him onto the cot and took off his shoes. "Don't worry about a thing. Celine will take care of you."

William leaned back and closed his eyes. She had finally managed to get him to stop talking about his precious Elizabeth for more than a minute.

"How about a nice foot rub?" she said in a baby voice.

"Hmmm . . ." William sighed.

That's more like it, Celine thought. It was about time he started paying attention to her. He wasted all his time fretting about Miss Goody-Goody, who didn't care about him at all, while Celine had to practically stand on her head for him to even notice she was in the room.

"Willie, why don't you come to my place for

dinner this week?" Celine said, her voice pure sugar. "I'll make some fried chicken and hush puppies. And I'll bake a nice peach pie for dessert. It's my granny's secret recipe," she drawled. "Doesn't that sound nice?"

William bolted upright. "You never quit, do you?" His ice-blue eyes glared at her. "How many times do I have to tell you that we can't be seen together? Don't ever bring that up again!"

"Sorry." Celine pouted as she watched William put his shoes back on. Why was he so tense?

He lit a cigarette. "I am too close to getting Elizabeth to let you mess it up for me." He blew a cloud of smoke into the air. "Don't you dare pull anything stupid."

Celine fluffed her hair. *William can be such a grouch,* she thought. "I don't know what you're talking about," she said stubbornly.

"You know exactly what I'm talking about," William answered. He walked over to Celine. "Go deliver that note like I told you," he said, pointing to the door. Celine didn't budge. "GET OUT!"

Damn him! Celine stomped out of the room. What made him think he could treat her this way, especially after everything she did for him?

She took the note he'd given her and ripped it into shreds. "You can do the dirty work yourself, Willie," she said as she threw it into the trash can. "I'm through with you."

*   *   *

Danny took off his tie and unbuttoned the top button of his shirt so he could breathe. He had been running all over campus looking for Isabella, but no one had seen her since late afternoon. *Maybe she's waiting in the tower,* he thought anxiously. He hated the thought of Isabella taking the elevator all the way up there to find only the mess he left behind. But before he went sprinting back to the tower, there was still one more place he had to check.

"Izzy, are you there?" he said as he lightly knocked on the door of her dorm room. He put his ear against the door but didn't hear anything.

Danny turned the knob and opened the door. His heartbeat was still pounding in his ears from the run. There was no sign of Isabella anywhere. The clothes she had worn that day were strewn over her desk chair, and her book bag was on the floor by her bed. Everything was exactly how it had been when he had come by earlier to drop off the note. Danny glanced at her pillow. The note and the rose were untouched.

Danny grabbed a few tissues from Isabella's bureau and wiped the sweat off his brow. If he didn't run into her around campus and she hadn't been to her room, then where was she? *It's like she dropped off the planet,* Danny thought as he took a seat on her bed. He untied his shoes. *She can't be far,* he figured. *We just keep getting our signals crossed.*

Danny stretched out on Isabella's bed. Lugging everything across campus to the library, setting it up, then dashing all over campus looking for Isabella had been tiring. There was no way he'd be able to dance until dawn in the state he was in. *I'll just take a little nap,* he thought, pulling the covers up to his chin. Isabella would wake him when she arrived.

It's not the most romantic way to start the evening, but it's better than bowling, Danny thought as he closed his eyes.

Chapter
Twelve

Jessica stepped out of Dickenson Hall into the bright sunlight. She headed toward the Perkins Building, where her English composition class was starting in five minutes. She hurried along the path so she wouldn't be late.

"Look who we have here," a voice said behind her. "It's Kiss-and-Tell Wakefield."

She turned. It was Peter Wilbourne and a few Sigmas. Peter was extremely powerful and was in the habit of always getting whatever or whoever he wanted—except for Jessica. She had refused to go out with him during the first few weeks of school, and since then, he'd pledged to make her life miserable.

Jessica faced forward and started walking faster. *Go away,* she thought. *Please, just leave me alone.*

They sped up too, and Jessica could feel Peter close behind. He bent down and whispered loudly in her ear, "Do you want to go out with me sometime? I hear you like to play rough."

One of the Sigmas laughed. "When you're done with him, you can go out with the rest of us."

Jessica continued to stare straight ahead, pretending to ignore the comments. She bit the insides of her cheeks so she wouldn't cry.

Peter put his arm around her. Jessica flinched. "You'd like that, wouldn't you?"

Jessica didn't speak. She wished she hadn't left the silver whistle in her room. She really needed it now.

"I don't hear you saying no, so I guess that means yes. Is that how it works, boys?" Peter asked.

"You know she likes it," one of them called.

Up ahead, coming toward them, was a group of Thetas. Mariela was among them. Jessica waved to get their attention, her eyes pleading to them for help. They turned their heads and walked by as if they had never seen her before in their lives.

"Looks like your friends are jealous," Peter said, stroking Jessica's hair.

Jessica's temper rose to its boiling point. "Leave me alone!" she yelled, loosening herself from Peter's grip. "All of you—just leave me alone!"

"Ooooh," called the chorus of Sigmas.

Jessica scrambled up the steps into the safety of Perkins. Tears streaked down her cheeks.

Isabella slammed the door to her Land-Rover and ran from the parking lot to her dorm. She had awoken from a peaceful sleep to the chirping of birds and the bright morning sunlight. It was wonderful for a brief moment—then she realized that Danny had never shown up last night.

She didn't know what to do first. After loading up the Land-Rover, she instinctively drove over to her dorm, thinking that Danny might have left a message on her answering machine.

Isabella opened the door to her room and threw her backpack onto the floor. She checked her answering machine, but there were no messages. *Maybe he's in his room.*

Isabella turned around to head out the door. Then out of the corner of her eye she spotted Danny. Actually she saw only the top of his head, because the rest of his body was buried under her floral comforter. "Danny?" she said as she edged closer to the bed. "Danny, wake up."

Danny opened his eyes and pushed aside the comforter. "Huh?" he answered groggily.

Isabella noticed that he was dressed in a black suit. Even though the suit was wrinkled and Danny was half asleep, he still looked gorgeous. She waited a moment for him to wake up. "What're you doing here?" she asked.

Danny rubbed his eyes. "Waiting for you." He stared at her flannel shirt and dirty jeans in disbelief.

"Why are you waiting for me here?" she asked, sitting on the edge of the bed. "The note said to meet me in the field. And why are you dressed like that?"

Danny shook his head and stared at her. "What note? What are you talking about?" He looked completely baffled. "What about the note I left you?" He motioned toward the end of the bed.

Isabella smiled when she saw the rose. She opened the note and read it to herself. "Oh, Danny," she said, throwing her arms around him. Isabella was stunned that he had gone to so much trouble for their anniversary. She'd have to take back everything she'd said about his being unromantic. This was the most romantic thing anyone had ever done for her.

"I saved you something." Danny smiled brightly as he reached in his pocket for the fortune cookie. But when he pulled out his hand, all that was left was a pile of crumbs with a slip of paper buried in it. "Sorry," he said, giving her the paper. "I must have rolled over it in my sleep."

"Danny, you're so sweet." Isabella gave him a kiss. "You *are* a romantic."

"I wish you'd been there," Danny said wistfully. "Where were you all this time?"

Isabella was so surprised by what Danny had done for her that she nearly forgot about her night in the field. "I had a little surprise of my own planned for our anniversary," she said as she pulled off her hiking boots. "I left you a note in your room, but I guess you never got it."

Danny shook his head. "I went straight from work to the tower." He put his arm around her. "So what was your surprise?"

"I planned an overnight camping trip for the two of us in the field behind the library."

"I should have guessed." Danny laughed as he touched her flannel shirt. He leaned forward and kissed her lightly on the lips. "Thank you."

"I spent the whole night out there, and believe it or not, I loved it. It was so peaceful. But you know what the best part of the whole thing was?"

"What?"

Isabella held up her hands. "I didn't break any nails." She laughed. "Do you want to go camping this weekend? I bought all this equipment, and I'd like to get a chance to use it. It'll be our real anniversary celebration."

"Actually, I was kind of hoping we could go back to the tower. The view is incredible," Danny said.

"Why not do both? If we have time left over, we can go bowling." Isabella smiled wryly. "That is, unless you're afraid of losing again."

Danny's eyes sparkled. "Is that a challenge?"

Jessica walked into her room and threw her book bag on the bed. This was definitely one of the worst days of her life.

She picked up the silver whistle that she'd left on her desk and attached it to her key chain. Even if she'd had it with her when the Sigmas were following her, she doubted it would have worked. The whole reason for carrying a whistle was so that other people could come to her aid. At the moment, that seemed useless. No one was on her side.

I hope Elizabeth's right, Jessica thought. *Maybe after the hearing, this will all blow over.*

Jessica was startled by a knock on the door. "Who is it?" she called.

There was no answer.

"Who is it?" Jessica repeated, louder this time. She put her ear up to the door.

"Jessica, open up. It's James."

Jessica froze. James was standing outside her door, expecting to come in. What was she going to do?

"I want to talk to you. Please, open the door." His voice sounded calm.

Maybe if I don't answer, he'll leave, she thought.

"Jess, come on."

He sounded sober. Jessica imagined what he looked like on the other side of the door. He probably just got out of practice, his hair still wet from taking a shower. His face tanned from outside practice. When he smiled, his eyes lit up. He looked so trustworthy. So safe.

"I just want to talk," he said.

Jessica reached to unlock the door, but she stopped herself. *No. Don't do it,* she told herself. *Don't let him in.*

"Jess, what are you doing? Why are you trying to ruin me?" he asked.

Ruin you? she thought incredulously. *How about me?*

"I thought you liked me. I thought things were going so well between us."

Me too. Jessica started to cry.

James paused for a moment. "Why did you betray me like that?"

Jessica felt rage burning inside her. What did James know about betrayal? *I'll tell you about betrayal,* she thought angrily. *Betrayal is when someone you trust turns into a drunken animal and tries to take advantage of you. When you tell them to stop and they go ahead anyway, pretending it's all a game.*

"GO AWAY!" Jessica screamed wildly. "I don't want to talk to you!"

"Just tell me why—"

"Get out of here before I call security!" She reached for the phone. She was halfway through dialing the number when she heard him walk away.

Jessica hung up the phone. When would all of this be over? At this rate, she wasn't sure she'd be able to last another day.

A few moments later the phone rang. Jessica was afraid to pick up the receiver. *It could be James,* she thought.

Or it could be Liz checking up on me. She lifted the receiver. "Hello?" she said timidly.

"Hello, Jess? It's Lila."

"Hey, Liz, wait up!" Maia yelled as she ran up the path. "I'm glad I caught you. I didn't want to carry this thing around all day."

Elizabeth took the book of Shakespeare's sonnets off her hands. "How did the paper go?"

"Pretty well, I think." She motioned toward a bench. "Can I talk to you for a minute?"

"Sure," Elizabeth answered. She had an hour before her next class. "What's up?"

Maia sat down. "I heard about Jessica pressing charges. She's doing such a brave thing. If there's anything I can do to help, please let me know."

"How about testifying at the hearing?" Elizabeth said bluntly.

Maia looked at the ground. "Believe it or not, I've thought about it," she said. "But I would probably fall apart in front of all those people—especially if I saw James. I'd end up hurting her case instead of helping it."

It seemed to Elizabeth that no amount of coaxing would get Maia to testify against James. Jessica would have to do it alone. "Why don't you at least stop by and see Jessica? She needs all the support she can get."

Maia shook her head. "I told you—I can't face her, Liz. I feel so guilty about what happened."

"Don't you understand? It's not your fault," Elizabeth said. She spoke forcefully. "James is the attacker—he's the one who should be feeling guilty. Not you."

"I know what you're saying. But it's not that easy—"

Elizabeth tried to control her anger. "Tell me something, Maia," she said. "If James isn't found guilty, what are you going to do? Are you going to continue to live in fear, hoping you don't run into

160

him or one of his friends? Are you going to let him control you for the rest of your college career?"

"That won't happen," Maia said, covering her face with her hands. "I'm planning to transfer to another school."

"It's so good to see you!" Lila squealed when she saw Jessica and Isabella walk through the door of her hospital room. They both gave her a hug.

"Hi, Mr. and Mrs. Fowler," Jessica greeted Lila's parents.

Mrs. Fowler gave her a hug. "If you hadn't called me that night, Jessica—" Her voice cracked. "I don't know when we would have realized that Lila was missing."

"I just wish I'd called you sooner," Jessica said. Tears welled up in her eyes.

"Come on, you two." Lila's own eyes were sparkling with tears. "Don't get me all worked up. Everything turned out fine."

"I know." Mrs. Fowler smiled, delicately dabbing the corners of her eyes.

"We're going to go get a cup of coffee so you can have some privacy," Mr. Fowler said. He gave his daughter a kiss on the cheek.

"Thanks." Lila kissed her mom good-bye. "If you pass Bruce's room, say hi for me," she called to them as they walked out the door.

Jessica took a seat on the edge of the bed. "This is for you from both of us." She glanced over at

Isabella. "Something to make your hospital stay a little bit more stylish."

Lila opened the decorated box. She pulled back the tissue paper and started to giggle. It was a red satin nightie with a matching robe. "Thanks, guys! I love it!"

"We couldn't bear the thought of you having to sleep in those awful hospital robes." Jessica made a face.

"I'm glad we didn't get flowers," Isabella commented. "You have so many bouquets, this place is starting to look like an English garden."

Lila smiled proudly. "Actually, there's more. My parents already took a carload home." Lila stared at her friends happily. It was great to be home.

"You look really good, Li. When can you leave?" Jessica asked.

"Pretty soon, I think. Maybe tomorrow." Lila's stomach did a flip. Twenty-four hours seemed like a lifetime. Tomorrow she would finally be with Bruce again.

"Are you going back to school right away?" Isabella asked, taking a seat on the other side of the bed.

Lila nodded. "I don't want to get too far behind. I already have a semester to make up as it is," she said. "So. What's new with you? What have I missed?"

Isabella and Jessica looked at each other. "Not much, really. I'll bore you when you get back," Jessica said, changing the subject. "Speaking of bores, what was it like being stranded in the wilderness with Bruce Patman?"

Lila flashed a one-hundred-megawatt smile.

"Uh-oh. I've seen that smile before," Jessica said knowingly.

Lila turned the voltage up another notch.

"I can't believe this. You didn't go and fall in love with him, did you?" Jessica rolled her eyes.

Lila thought back to the night before they were rescued. She remembered how Bruce had given her his shirt so she wouldn't freeze. Jessica and Isabella would never understand it, but she had seen the real Bruce. "He's not like you think," Lila said dreamily. "We went through a lot together. When you're in a desperate situation, you really get to know a person."

"Desperate is right," Jessica said dryly. She turned to Isabella playfully. "Doctor, please check this patient for brain damage."

Isabella felt Lila's forehead. "She seems all right to me." She smiled. "Although she may be experiencing a little dizziness."

"I'm serious," Lila protested. "He was really sweet. When we were hiking through the forest, he cut down branches out of my way. He took clothes off his own back so I could stay warm. He even went fishing so we could eat."

Jessica looked at Isabella with surprise. "Maybe we should be checking Bruce for brain damage."

"Ha ha," Lila said. They could make fun all they

wanted; it didn't matter to her. "Bruce is a great guy—trust me."

"I'm sorry," Jessica said, her laughter subsiding. "I think it's great you two got along so well. It's just hard to believe, that's all."

"Are you two going to be an item now that you're home?" Isabella asked.

Lila sighed. "I hope so."

Chapter Thirteen

"Hi, Alex."

Alex whirled around to see Todd Wilkins standing in the checkout line of the campus bookstore. She hadn't seen him in a few days, and he looked good. His face didn't have that same tired, drawn look that it had when he was drinking heavily. Maybe he had stopped for good.

"What's up, Todd?" she asked as she casually rifled through a bin full of felt-tipped pens.

He waved a notebook at her awkwardly. "Just getting some things for my classes."

She nodded politely. It was strange not having anything to say to someone she had shared so much with. But Todd was part of the past. She was ready to move on.

"So, are you seeing anybody?" Todd shifted from one foot to the other.

"Uh . . ." Alex stalled. She didn't want to tell

him about her feelings for Noah. "Not really. How about you?"

Todd looked at the floor. "Not at the moment," he said shyly.

Alex felt a dull ache in her stomach. Todd seemed incredibly lonely—but she didn't feel like there was anything she could do to help. It was hard to believe that she'd actually wanted to be his girlfriend.

Alex glanced over to the door, where she saw Noah walking into the store. Her heart leapt for joy as she watched him look at a display of books. She wanted to wave her hands and call his name, but she just stood there, watching.

A minute passed, then Noah spotted her. His face lit up, and he walked over to where she was standing.

"Hi, Alex," he said brightly. He looked as though he was about to delve into some deep, involved conversation with her when he noticed Todd standing nearby. His smile faded, then he looked back and forth between the two of them.

"Noah, have you met Todd?" Alex said haltingly as she noticed his swift change in mood.

"No, I haven't. Nice to meet you," Noah said stiffly. Todd nodded. Noah scanned the bookstore as if to find something that could take him away from the awkwardness of the situation. "Well, I have some books to buy. I'll talk to you later," he said before sprinting to the psychology aisle.

"He seems like a nice guy," Todd said as he handed his money to the cashier.

Alex nodded. She looked for Noah, but he was still out of sight. *He doesn't think I'm still interested in Todd, does he?* Alex was worried that Noah had misunderstood.

"Well, it was good to see you," Todd said, taking his bag.

"It was nice to see you, too," she said. "I'll see you around."

Jessica shifted uneasily in her chair as she watched the three judges sitting across from her. Even though it was only a trial run and the three faces in front of her belonged to Elizabeth, Steven, and Billie, she still felt nervous. If she felt this anxious sitting in Steven and Billie's kitchen, Jessica couldn't imagine what it would be like at the real hearing.

"Are you ready, Jess?" Steven handed Billie and Elizabeth slips of paper with writing on them. "We're going to ask some questions that the disciplinary committee might ask you at the hearing. It'll give you a chance to get your thoughts together."

Billie lightly touched Jessica's hand. "Some of the questions are going to be tough. Just do the best you can. We'll guide you through it."

Jessica nodded. "Fire away."

"You start, Liz," Steven said.

Elizabeth read from her slip of paper. "What were you wearing the night of the attack?"

Jessica stared at her sister. "This is a hearing, not

a fashion show," she said with exasperation. "That's not fair."

"It doesn't matter; they could ask you anyway," said Steven.

Jessica folded her arms across her chest. "I just won't answer, then."

Elizabeth made a buzzer sound. "Wrong answer. Being stubborn isn't going to work this time. You have to be cooperative, or they'll sympathize with James. You know how charming he can be."

Jessica frowned. "What am I going to say, then? I was wearing a red bustier top and black silk pants. Not the most conservative outfit."

Billie set a pitcher of iced tea on the table. "Why not say that you were wearing pants and a top? It's the truth, isn't it? I don't see why you have to go into details, since it's not a fair question anyway."

Steven poured himself a glass of tea. "Try this one: Did you make it clear to him that you didn't want sex?"

"I said no many times."

"At what point did you say no?"

"Steven! What kind of question is that?" Jessica was growing more and more worried. If these were the kinds of questions they were going to ask at the hearing, she didn't want to be there.

Elizabeth looked sympathetically at her sister. "We're just trying to prepare you. Don't get upset."

"How can I answer that? I was saying no the whole time," Jessica answered.

"Then that's exactly what you say. You said no from the very beginning," Steven prompted.

Billie took a sip of tea. "It's going to seem embarrassing at times, but you have to just tell them what happened. Be straightforward. You're the one who's right—just remember that. You have nothing to be ashamed of."

"It's going to be his word against yours," Elizabeth said. "James is going to be real cool, so you're going to have to keep yourself together."

Jessica's mind was spinning. How was she supposed to remember everything they were telling her? She imagined herself in front of the committee members and the whole school, completely paralyzed with fear, unable to speak.

"I don't want to scare you," Steven said. "But you need to know what you're up against."

"I wish you had told me all this at the beginning, so I wouldn't have pressed charges. I could've saved myself a lot of grief," Jessica answered. Her head was pounding.

"Just relax, you'll be great," Billie said with optimism.

Jessica stood up. "Can we take a little break? I need some air . . ."

"Sure." Elizabeth looked worried. "Do you want me to come with you?"

"No—thanks anyway." Jessica slipped out of the door and down the steps. She opened the front door of the apartment building and sat on the stoop.

169

Jessica closed her eyes and rested her head on her knees. The air was soothing, and her head began to clear. It still wasn't too late to back out. All she'd have to do was call the committee and say she'd made a mistake. It would be so easy. Of course, she'd have to transfer to another school—there was no way she could stay after that. But that would be all right. With all that had happened since the beginning of school, Jessica was ready for a fresh start.

She took a deep breath, noticing the familiar scent of worn leather in the air. Then she heard the soft thud of someone sitting down beside her. "Hi, Jess," he said.

Jessica looked up. It had been so long since she had seen those warm, golden eyes. Instead of feeling upset, she was strangely comforted. "Hi, Mike," she answered.

"Are you OK?" he asked quietly. "You look a little upset."

"I'm all right." She looked at the cane in his hand and felt a pang of sadness. "How are you?"

"I'm getting around OK." He smiled. "I'll be back to normal in no time."

Seeing Mike dredged up so many memories for her. She wished she could slip back to the days when they had just been married and everything seemed so perfect. Jessica longed for the days filled with motorcycle trips through Nevada and the nights sleeping under desert stars. She would have given anything to relive just one day, to not have any cares—to be in love again. But that time had passed. It was over.

"Good luck at the hearing tomorrow," Mike said, interrupting her thoughts.

Jessica looked at him with surprise. "How did you know? Steven didn't tell you, did he?"

Mike shook his head. "No, Steven didn't say a word. It's a small town; word gets around."

The thought that everyone in town knew about it made Jessica feel even worse. "Do you know who it was?" she asked cautiously.

"Yeah. I know his name. Don't worry, I'm not going to do anything about it."

Jessica was relieved. The last thing she wanted was to get Mike involved. "Thanks."

Mike sighed. "Believe me, I wanted to go after the guy, but I decided that it was your battle to fight. I realized that when I let you go—" He broke off for a moment. "That I had to let you go completely. As much as I hate it, I have to stay out of your life."

Jessica blinked back a tear. Something had changed in Mike since the accident. He'd matured. "Thank you," she said gratefully. "Thanks for understanding."

Mike leaned over and kissed her gently on the forehead. "You go to that hearing tomorrow and show that sleaze who's boss." Mike got to his feet.

"OK," Jessica said hoarsely. She smiled.

"Anytime you need anything, you know where I am," he said. Mike slowly climbed the steps and went into the building.

"Yeah," Jessica whispered as he closed the door.

"Look at that bouquet!" Mrs. Fowler exclaimed as the nurse entered, carrying a crystal vase filled with red roses. "It's absolutely stunning."

Lila's stomach did a somersault. The flowers were so elegant and so beautiful, they had to be from Bruce.

"What does the card say?"

Lila opened the tiny envelope. "Glad to hear you're fine. Get well soon. Love, Aunt Irma and Uncle Richard." Her heart sank.

"How nice of them," Mrs. Fowler said, placing the vase on the hospital nightstand.

Lila tried not to let her disappointment show. But it was difficult. Even though he was right down the hall from her, Lila hadn't seen Bruce since the rescue. She had been bombarded with visiting relatives and friends, making it impossible for her to break away for even ten minutes. It was probably the same for him.

"I suppose we ought to leave before your father gets too comfortable," Mrs. Fowler said, motioning to Mr. Fowler, who was dozing softly in a chair. "Besides, visiting hours are almost over."

Lila perked up a bit. Once her parents left, she would be completely, totally alone. She imagined how great it would be to sneak into Bruce's room and surprise him. "I'm *so* tired," Lila said with a fake yawn. She thought it might speed up her parents' exit.

"Should we take some more flowers home?" her mother asked.

"Please do." Lila watched anxiously as her mother looked over each bouquet, stopping occasionally to rearrange flowers or pull out a few of the wilted blossoms. It was driving her crazy. Now that she realized she might get some time alone with Bruce, she was growing impatient. It was funny how she had spent nearly a week with him, alone in the wilderness, hating nearly every moment of it. And now that they were safely back in Sweet Valley, she couldn't stand to be away. Lila laughed.

"What's so funny, dear?" Mrs. Fowler said.

Lila tried to control her giggling. "Nothing, really. I guess I'm just overtired."

Lila's mother woke up Mr. Fowler and handed him a basket of orchids. "We're leaving so you can get your rest," she said. "Give us a call tomorrow morning, so we know when we can pick you up." Lila kissed them both and waved good-bye as they walked out the door.

Alone at last. Lila sighed. She wondered if Bruce was sitting in his room, surrounded by boring relatives but thinking about her the whole time. Or he could be alone, waiting for her to stop by. "There's only one way to find out," Lila said aloud as she wrapped herself in her new satin robe. She couldn't stand another minute without him.

She walked down the corridor, squinting from the bright fluorescent lights. She found Bruce's room at the end of the hall near the stairwell. His door was half open.

The light inside the room was dim. From where she stood in the doorway, the room looked empty. She gently eased open the door.

"Bruce?" she called softly as she entered. The TV was on. Bruce's feet and head were propped up by pillows and his arms were bandaged where he had been cut. He was sound asleep.

Lila tiptoed to the edge of the bed. He looked so innocent and peaceful. He had a boyish quality that reminded her so much of Tisiano that she suddenly felt tears come to her eyes. What was going on inside his head? *Is he dreaming about me?*

Unfortunately, she had no way of knowing. She didn't even know if he still cared about her. As much as she hoped that they would be together when they returned to the university, she had to face the fact that there weren't any guarantees.

Lila leaned over his bed and kissed him softly on the forehead. He stirred a little but didn't wake up. She turned off the television set, then slipped back into the bright corridor.

"Oh, no! Look at this," Jessica called to Elizabeth. "We must have run over a nail."

Elizabeth hurried over to the other side of the Jeep, where Jessica stood. They had gone to see a late movie to get Jessica's mind off the hearing. Elizabeth looked at the tire. Sticking out of it was a long nail. The tire was completely flat. *Why did this have to happen now?* she thought nervously.

"The funny thing is, I don't remember driving over it," Jessica said.

Elizabeth's heart was pounding in her throat. Was this some sort of trick? She stared at the trees that lined the edge of the empty parking lot, trying to see if anyone was watching.

"Well, we've got the spare on the back," Jessica said tiredly. "Do you remember how to change a tire? I know Dad showed us, but I wasn't paying much attention."

Elizabeth found the jack and the tire iron in the back. The lights of the parking lot were dim. Elizabeth felt as though the darkness was closing in on her. "You take the spare tire off the back," Elizabeth ordered. She inserted the tire iron and tried to turn it, but the lug nuts wouldn't budge.

In the distance she could hear a truck approaching. Her palms started to sweat, and her hands couldn't grip the tire iron. "Come on!" she shouted furiously at the tire iron. Her hands were sore. The truck turned the corner and pulled up beside the Jeep, its flashing yellow lights reflecting off the pavement.

Elizabeth looked up. The tow truck was black, with yellow and green stripes. Just like the one that almost towed her off campus. *Come on!* Elizabeth thought anxiously. Why weren't the lug nuts turning? She heard the slam of the truck door and the footsteps of the driver approaching.

"Is either one of you Jessica Wakefield?" the driver of the tow truck asked. Elizabeth looked at him. It wasn't the same driver she'd seen the other night. This man had a kindly face and a friendly smile.

"I am," Jessica said, looking confused.

How did he know we were in trouble? Elizabeth wondered. She felt the tiny hairs on the back of her neck stand up.

He looked at the tire. "I got a call that someone by the name of Jessica Wakefield needed help, but they didn't mention what the trouble was."

"We ran over a nail," Elizabeth said. "Who called?"

"He didn't give us a name," the driver said.

Jessica and Elizabeth looked at each other. They were in a deserted parking, all alone. Who could have made that call?

"Looks like you have a good start on this," he said as he tried to loosen the nuts.

"They wouldn't come off," said Elizabeth.

"It's those darn pneumatic wrenches. Next time you get your tires rotated, ask them to tighten the nuts by hand." The driver stomped on the end of the tire iron, and the lugs magically loosened.

Elizabeth couldn't shake the strange feeling she had. She could feel someone nearby—watching every move they made.

"How much do we owe you?" Jessica asked when he was done.

The driver shook his head. "Nothing—it's already

been taken care of. Have a good night, ladies."

Elizabeth was already in the passenger's seat, buckled in and ready to go. *Hurry, Jess,* she thought impatiently. *Let's get out of here.* . . . Out of the corner of her eye, Elizabeth saw something moving by the trees. She turned her head just in time to catch a glimpse of the figure as it slid back into the shadows.

Chapter
Fourteen

Jessica stood in front of her full-length mirror, holding a purple skirt against her body. "Too short," she said with a sigh. She tossed the skirt onto the growing pile on the floor. She had tried on nearly all the clothes in her closet. It seemed that everything she owned was too revealing.

"Not the right impression to give the disciplinary committee." Jessica searched through her twin's closet. Elizabeth always had plenty of conservative clothes. After a few moments Jessica chose a beige, knee-length linen skirt and a plain white button-down blouse.

Jessica changed her clothes. It was amazing how much she looked like Elizabeth when she wore Elizabeth's clothes. She even started acting like her. Maybe if she felt like Elizabeth, she'd be able to handle the committee's questions with as much composure as her sister could. She buttoned the top button of the blouse.

There was a soft knock at the door. "Who is it?" Jessica asked cautiously.

"It's Maia."

Jessica opened the door. "Come on in. Elizabeth is still in class. She won't be back for another half hour."

"That's all right," Maia said. "I came to see you."

Jessica offered her a seat. She was shocked to see Maia, but she tried to appear casual. "What's up, Maia?"

"I wanted to wish you luck today at the hearing." Her voice was quiet, and she stared at the floor. "I think you're very courageous to confront James."

Jessica smiled sadly. It was nice to hear words of encouragement.

"I wish I could have done the same thing," Maia said.

"Don't beat yourself up, Maia. Everyone deals with things differently. Remember, Elizabeth came to my rescue in time—but James raped you. Your scars run much deeper than mine."

Maia started to cry. "Oh, Jessica, I'm *so* sorry. I could have prevented all this if only I had done something about it. Look what I've put you through."

Jessica felt her own eyes grow damp. She had cried so much lately that she was surprised she had any tears left. "You did the best you could."

Maia looked up for the first time. Reflected in her hazel eyes was the same pain and guilt that Jessica recognized in herself.

"I can't testify today," insisted Maia. "I want to help you—but I can't do it."

"I understand." Jessica was disappointed. But as much as she needed her, it was Maia's right not to testify if she didn't want to. "Liz might not see your point of view clearly, but I do." Jessica gave Maia a hug, partly to comfort her and partly to ward off her own feeling of dread.

"Thanks," Maia said softly.

Jessica pulled back after a few moments, brushing away a tear. "So, what do you think?" She tried to lighten the mood. "Is this outfit OK for the hearing?"

"Very nice," Maia said. "Although—" She studied Jessica for a moment, then reached over and unbuttoned the top button of her blouse. "There's no use in choking yourself." She smiled. "And maybe you need an accessory to perk it up just a bit." Maia took off the printed scarf that was around her neck and tied it on Jessica. "For good luck," she said.

Alex was lying on her bed, staring at the phone. She couldn't decide whom to call. One side of her wanted to call Noah, to make sure he didn't think she was still interested in Todd. She also wanted to see if he would ask her out on a real date—dinner and a movie would be nice. But what if Noah rejected her?

The other side of her wished she could call T-Squared. He'd give her the confidence she needed. But she was afraid to call him, too. All she'd have to do was hear the sound of his voice, and she'd fall for him all over again.

The phone rang. *Looks like the decision has been made for me,* she thought as she picked up the phone. "Hello?"

"Who am I speaking with?" a voice asked.

Alex gasped. She recognized that voice. "T-Squared, is that you?" *How did he get my number?* she wondered.

There was a brief period of silence. "Alex, this is Noah."

Alex had never felt so happy and so disappointed at the same time. "I'm sorry," she said, slightly embarrassed. "You sounded like a friend of mine."

"It's OK," he answered. "I didn't have a chance to talk to you in the bookstore, and I wanted to find out how you did on the exam."

Alexandra twirled the telephone cord around her fingers. "Pretty well. I surprised myself," she said. "But I couldn't have done it without you."

"It was my pleasure." There was an awkward silence, then he spoke. "Alex, I was wondering if you'd like to go out tonight."

"Let me see . . ." *He asked me out again!* Alex danced around her room excitedly. "Sure, that would be fine," she answered, trying to sound cool.

"How about seven? In front of the coffeehouse."

"I'll be there," she answered.

*   *   *

"Just stop at the front desk to sign the release form, and then you're free to go," the nurse said as she changed the bedsheets for the next patient.

Lila brushed her hair and gathered her clothes. It was finally time to leave. She remembered that she was supposed to call her parents so they could pick her up, but Lila decided to wait and call them when she got back to the university. She'd fantasized a lot about her reunion with Bruce, and she didn't want people around to spoil it.

"Excuse me," Lila said eagerly to the nurse. "Could you please tell me how Bruce Patman is doing? When is he scheduled to leave?"

The nurse paused. "Actually, he was released about twenty minutes ago."

Lila's heart sank. Was it possible that Bruce would leave without coming to see her? *There must be some mistake,* she thought. *This can't be true.*

She grabbed her bag and ran out into the corridor. Maybe there was a chance he was still in the building. He might even be waiting for her at the nurses' station, ready to take her in his arms, just like she'd dreamed.

Her eyes scanned the corridor, but Bruce was nowhere in sight. *What were you thinking?* Lila asked herself. Suddenly her fantasies seemed foolish. Of course things between them weren't going to be the same after the rescue. How could she have been so naive?

Lila signed the release form. A candy striper

brought a wheelchair for her and wheeled her to the main entrance, where a cab was waiting.

Maybe he's in the cab, Lila hoped, not daring to look. It wasn't until the cabby opened the door for her that Lila raised her eyes. The backseat was empty.

Jessica couldn't stop fidgeting. "I want to go home, Liz," she whispered to her twin. The room was packed with students who had come to watch the hearing.

Elizabeth rested her hand on Jessica's shoulder. "The hearing is going to start any minute. Just try to relax. Remember what we told you last night."

Remember? Jessica had had trouble taking it all in as they coached her. *There's no way I'm going to remember anything in front all these people,* she thought miserably.

Elizabeth seemed to read her thoughts. "Just stay calm and be straightforward and honest. Don't argue—just tell them your side of the story."

Jessica's hands were ice cold. "Lizzie—I'm scared."

"I know," Elizabeth answered sympathetically. "But just think of all the people who are here to support you."

Jessica turned around. Several rows of folded chairs were lined up behind her, and nearly all of them were filled with friends who had come to give her encouragement. Jessica nodded weakly at the

Thetas who'd been supporting her. Denise Waters waved. "Good luck, Jess," she mouthed. Isabella and Danny ran up and gave Jessica a quick hug. Steven and Billie were sitting directly behind her, whispering words of encouragement. Tears came to Jessica's eyes when she recognized the faces of some of the women she had met at the march. They were there for her, too.

But her confidence quickly deflated when she looked at the other side of the room. The Sigmas had come to support James, all decked out in their blue fraternity jackets. Peter Wilbourne stared directly at Jessica, his eyes boring through her. Panic hit her like an electric shock, and she quickly looked away. Jessica spotted Alison and Mariela sitting close to the front, behind James. Alison shot Jessica a hostile look.

The committee filed into the room and seated themselves at a long table in the front of the room. The committee was made up of four faculty members and four students, an equal ratio of male to female. Their faces were stern and serious.

Jessica stared straight ahead, waiting for the hearing to begin. She still hadn't looked at James, who was sitting only a few feet away from her. She wondered if he was as nervous as she was.

"If I could have your attention, please," said Mr. Shreeve, the dean of students. "If you could all come to order, we're ready to start."

The crowd settled down. "You can do it,"

Elizabeth whispered in Jessica's ear just before she took her seat.

"Let's begin," Dean Shreeve said. He then introduced all the members of the committee. "Ms. Wakefield, you have registered a complaint with this committee involving Mr. James Montgomery. Is this correct?"

Jessica opened her mouth to speak, but it felt as though it was stuffed with cotton. "Yes," she finally answered.

"And what is the charge you are making against Mr. Montgomery?"

Jessica's face reddened. She felt the weight of everyone's stares. "Sexual assault."

"Ms. Wakefield," Dean Shreeve said. "Do you realize the seriousness of this charge? Are you aware that your accusation could have a profound effect on Mr. Montgomery's reputation?"

Out of the corner of her eye, Jessica saw James turn to her. Her hands began to shake. "Yes, I'm aware."

"Then you wish to continue with this hearing?"

Jessica thought about what the dean was saying. He was giving her a chance to back out. One little word, and she could go home and forget everything. It would be so easy. She looked at Elizabeth, who was nodding at her. Jessica turned to the committee. "Yes, I want to continue," she said.

"All right, then," the dean said. He pulled a piece of paper out of a folder and looked it over. "In your complaint," he said, referring to the piece of paper in his hand, "it states that you were dating Mr. Montgomery, and that the attack occurred one evening when you were out together. Could you please describe in detail what happened that night?"

Jessica took a deep breath and gripped the edges of her chair. *Be strong,* she told herself. She wished she still felt as invincible and confident as she did the night of the march. Jessica closed her eyes and tried to envision the crowd chanting, the candles, the energy all around her.

"Ms. Wakefield, we're waiting," the dean said. Someone in the back of the room snickered.

Jessica opened her eyes. "Yes, I'm sorry," she said softly. *This is it.* "On the night of the attack, James took me to the Mountain Lodge Inn." The first few words were the hardest, but as she began to describe the attack, Jessica felt the words pouring out of her. It was as if they were coming out all by themselves.

". . . After dinner, James drove us to Lookout Point. I didn't want him to, because he had had too much to drink. I even tried to take the keys away from him, but he wouldn't let me. . . ."

You're doing fine, Jessica thought as she heard herself continue with the story. The committee members were listening intently as she spoke, taking notes at important points. Jessica gained more confidence.

". . . My sister Elizabeth managed to get me out

of James's car and into the Jeep. We took off before he had a chance to follow us," Jessica finished.

Dean Shreeve made a note. "Is there anything else you'd like to add before we begin the questioning?" he asked.

Jessica thought over what she had just said, making sure she hadn't left anything out. "No, I don't think so," Jessica said. "That's everything."

"OK, now we'll open the hearing to questions from the committee members," the dean said.

Jessica tried to remain calm, hoping she would do better than she had at Steven's.

"Is there anyone who would like to start?" he asked.

"I have a question," said one of the male students. He wore a dark-blue necktie and a white dress shirt with the sleeves rolled to his elbows. "Did you ever go out with Mr. Montgomery before the night of the attack?"

"Yes. We went out several times."

"Did he ever make any sexual comments to you—or any unwelcome advances?"

Jessica released her grip on the chair and placed her hands in her lap. It was a straightforward question. She hoped they'd all be that way. "Yes. One night at a fraternity party, he took me outside, away from everyone, and tried to . . . to put his hands up my shirt," Jessica stumbled. "I yelled at him to stop and he wouldn't. Luckily someone walked in on us."

The student rhythmically tapped the table with

the end of his pencil. "If Mr. Montgomery made unwanted sexual advances toward you at a party, why did you go out with him again?"

Jessica's body tensed. How could she explain it? It was a question she had asked herself so many times. "He'd been drinking that night . . . I thought he was just acting that way because he was drunk . . . I didn't think he'd do it again."

Several committee members jotted down notes. Jessica desperately wished she could see what they were writing. "Ms. Wakefield," another committee member said. She was a young student with glasses. Jessica thought she had a kind face. "Did you say or do anything that could possibly have led Mr. Montgomery to believe that you wanted to have sex with him?"

Jessica shook her head. "No—I made it clear to him that I didn't want to have sex."

"Are you sure?" the student asked carefully. "Think back—is there anything you could have done that might have been misinterpreted?"

Jessica thought about Alison, who had accused her of leading James on from the very start. Jessica could feel the anger that Alison had provoked that afternoon in the Theta parlor. "No," Jessica answered firmly.

"Yeah, right!" someone in the back of the room shouted sarcastically. Jessica's face burned.

"If anyone speaks out again, I will clear this room," Dean Shreeve said severely. He turned to the committee. "Please continue."

"Are you certain he intended to rape you?" asked a male faculty member Jessica didn't recognize.

What kind of question is that? Jessica thought. "I don't understand the question," she said.

"Well, you said that he was rough with you and he touched you, but that your sister arrived before Mr. Montgomery went any further." He stared at her over the top of his reading glasses. "So, in effect, you really don't know if he would have raped you."

But I do know, Jessica thought, touching the scarf around her neck. Maia was the key to everything—the only proof she had of James's intent—but she couldn't tell them. "No, I don't have any absolute proof that he wanted to rape me—I can't read his mind. But when he was hitting me and dragging me toward the car, I knew it wasn't his way of being romantic," she answered, her voice taking on a bitter edge.

"Ms. Wakefield, please refrain from making sarcastic comments," Dean Shreeve said.

Good going. Jessica was certain that she had just ruined any chance she had of proving her case. "I'm sorry," she said quietly.

Another female student on the committee spoke. "When he was 'dragging' and 'hitting' you, as you put it, did you fight back? Did you tell him to stop?"

How could she ask such an idiotic question? Jessica had already told them that she did. Her emotions tempted her to lash out with a biting comment, but reason kept her in check. "Of course, I did what I could, but look at him—" She pointed to where James was sitting. "He's a star athlete. I didn't have a chance against someone his size."

The committee members were quiet for a moment. A few seemed lost in thought; others were scribbling furiously in their notebooks.

"Any more questions?" the dean asked.

"I have a few questions," a female faculty member asked. Jessica recognized her as Celeste Jenkins, a professor of psychology. "Is it true that you're recently divorced?"

Jessica was bewildered. *What did Mike have to do with this?* "My marriage was annulled," she said, trying to control her voice, which was shaking with anger. "Could you please tell me what this has to do with the attack?"

"Isn't it possible that your failed marriage has left you feeling bitter toward men?"

Jessica felt Elizabeth's hand on her shoulder, trying to calm her down. *Why is she mentioning my personal life?* "I am *not* going to discuss my marriage in front of this committee," Jessica answered firmly. "It has nothing to do with the attack, and I refuse to answer any questions about it!" The anger was beginning to show in her voice.

"Ms. Wakefield!" Dean Shreeve said harshly. "I have already warned you once. If you continue to respond in this manner, I'm going to throw out your complaint."

A wave of nausea hit her. Jessica felt as though things were quickly slipping out of her control. James sat in the same relaxed position as before, his face filled with smug satisfaction. Things weren't going well for her, and he obviously knew it.

Chapter
Fifteen

"Is anyone here?" Bruce shouted after banging several times on the bell near the cash register. The flower shop was completely quiet and in perfect order, like a museum.

I hope Lila hasn't left yet, Bruce thought anxiously. He knew he should have checked in on her first, but he really wanted to surprise her with a bouquet of flowers. *Who are you trying to fool, Patman?* he thought. *Lila's had enough time alone to remember what a jerk you've been all these years. She'll probably tell you she changed her mind. . . .*

Maybe flowers weren't such a good idea, after all. *This is a mistake,* Bruce thought as he turned and started to walk out of the shop. The door behind the counter squeaked open.

"May I help you, young man?" an elderly woman asked. "I'm sorry to keep you waiting. I was busy taking orders over the phone. We've had an unusual number of funerals this week."

I'm glad mine wasn't one of them, Bruce thought soberly. "Yes—could I have a dozen long-stemmed champagne roses?" The words had slipped out so easily, Bruce hardly realized what he had done. Lila was going to get flowers whether she wanted them or not.

"Do you want them in a box or wrapped in paper?"

"Whatever's quicker. I'm in a hurry."

"That would be a box. I don't have to take the time to arrange them. . . . Is this for a special young lady?" the woman asked cheerfully.

Bruce paced the floor. "She's very special," he said, trying not to sound as impatient as he felt.

"In that case, I'll put a bow on the box. What do you think of this one?" She held up a spool of forest-green velvet ribbon.

"Lovely," Bruce said dryly. At this very moment, Lila could be searching for him. If she found out that he'd already been released and that he'd left without saying good-bye . . . she'd give up on him for sure.

"Almost finished . . . Oh, dear me," she said as the bow unraveled. "I can't seem to tie these as easily as I used to."

"Let me help." Bruce grabbed the ends of the ribbon.

The elderly woman guided him through the steps. "Now tuck that piece under . . . that's right . . . fold the end over . . . now pull. What a splendid bow!"

Even Bruce had to admit that it turned out pretty well. He hoped Lila would appreciate it. That was, if he could get to her in time.

He quickly paid for the flowers and hurried out of the flower shop. "Thanks!" he shouted over his shoulder.

"Good luck with the young lady!" the woman called after him.

Luck. That's exactly what I need . . . and lots of it, Bruce thought as he ran toward the hospital.

"Elizabeth Wakefield—would you please tell the committee what you saw when you arrived at Lookout Point?" the dean asked.

Elizabeth nodded. "When I stopped the Jeep, I heard Jessica screaming, but I couldn't see her because they were in the car. I walked over to the car and looked in the window. That's when I saw James on top of her, and Jessica trying to fight him off."

"And how did you react when you saw this?" the dean asked.

Elizabeth's stomach churned as she remembered that horrible night. "My first instinct was to get her out of the car . . ." Elizabeth stopped. How would the committee react when they heard that she smashed the windshield of James's car? She decided that it was better that she tell the story, instead of leaving it for James to tell. Then she'd look like a liar. ". . . so I grabbed a tire iron and broke the windshield—"

"Wait a minute," the male professor interrupted. "Are you saying that you smashed Mr. Montgomery's car? Why such a drastic measure? You could have at least tried to talk to him first."

"There wasn't any time," Elizabeth answered firmly. She knew it sounded extreme, but Elizabeth was confident that she had handled it the best way she knew how. "Besides, the doors were locked. I had to get his attention." Students in the back of the room whispered among themselves. One of the male students on the committee stared at Elizabeth like she was a lunatic.

"Once I broke the glass, I reached in and unlocked the door," she continued, unfazed by the reactions around her. "Then I helped Jessica get away from James."

A female faculty member smiled politely at Elizabeth. "It's still not clear to me why you were there," she said. "How did you know that your sister was being attacked?"

"Someone told me," Elizabeth answered.

"Who told you?" a male student asked.

Elizabeth looked down. *Maia—if only you were here,* she thought. But she wasn't. Elizabeth glanced at her sister. Jessica's eyes reflected the same turmoil that Elizabeth was feeling—she was torn between revealing Maia's name and protecting her. Elizabeth turned back to the committee. Just as she was about to speak, Jessica tapped her on the shoulder. All it took was one look at her twin's face, and Elizabeth knew that she had finally made her decision. Jessica wanted to keep Maia out of it.

Elizabeth cleared her throat. "I can't say."

"Why not?" the student asked, his tone sarcastic.

Elizabeth stood her ground. "I don't want this person to be involved."

"Ms. Wakefield—" .Dean Shreeve interjected. "You realize that it's difficult for this committee to take your testimony into consideration if your answers are vague."

"I realize that," Elizabeth said resolutely. "But I'm sorry—I can't be more specific."

The male professor shifted uncomfortably in his chair. He seemed irritated. "You work for WSVU as a reporter, don't you?"

"Yes," Elizabeth answered. *What is he getting at?* she wondered, trying to anticipate his next question.

"And I noticed that you organized that women's march—you're very involved in women's rights, aren't you?"

"Yes." There was a tingling sensation crawling up her spine, and Elizabeth had the feeling that he was about to take a shot at her.

The professor folded his hands and leaned forward. "Isn't it possible that you and your sister are doing this as a publicity stunt? This would make a good story for WSVU, wouldn't it?"

"Absolutely not!" Elizabeth shouted. The room was buzzing with conversation.

"Quiet, please!" the dean called.

Elizabeth looked at her sister. The corners of Jessica's mouth trembled, and she looked as though she was about to burst into tears at any moment. Elizabeth wasn't too far from crying herself. At first, she'd felt like she was doing such a good job of defending her sister. Now, in a matter of minutes, they had managed to make her look like a publicity-starved psycho. Elizabeth tapped her feet restlessly. *How can I argue against that*? she wondered. Her mind went blank.

"Thank you, Ms. Wakefield," Dean Shreeve said. "If there aren't any more questions, I'd like to move on to Mr. Montgomery's testimony."

When the room quieted down, they continued. Jessica watched James. He sat up in his chair and straightened his tie. He looked great—very confident. The committee members turned to him, and James flashed his most charming smile.

"Mr. Montgomery, please tell the committee your side of the story," Dean Shreeve said.

Jessica shifted uncomfortably in her seat, anxiety gnawing at her insides. What would he tell them?

"First of all," James began, looking directly at the committee, "I just want to say that all of this is a big misunderstanding." He ran his fingers through his hair. The room was completely silent. "Everything that Jessica said about our date was completely true—up until the part about Lookout Point."

"What do you disagree with?" asked the dean.

198

James crossed his arms in front of his chest and leaned back in his chair. "The fact is, things were going great until her sister showed up. Jessica did seem a little reluctant at first, but she quickly warmed up to the idea."

"You mean of having sex?" one of the female professors asked.

James nodded. "Yes. The next thing I know, Elizabeth is smashing my windshield. She was screaming and hollering at me, and then she pulled Jessica out of the car. After that they took off."

The female student glared at James. "Are you saying that you think Elizabeth took Jessica away against her will?"

"I don't know for sure, but it seems that way to me." He looked over at Elizabeth. Jessica lowered her head to avoid his gaze. "I have a feeling that Elizabeth is overprotective of her sister. If Jessica wanted to leave, she would have done it on her own."

How could I, when you were holding me down? Jessica screamed in her head. How could he talk about Elizabeth that way? Jessica turned to her twin. Elizabeth's jaw was set, and her knuckles were white as she clenched her fists. She looked as if she was about to lunge at James.

"Mr. Montgomery," the female professor continued, "if you believe that Elizabeth took her sister away from you, isn't it likely that Jessica would have come back to you later on, of her own free will?"

James shook his head, as if the whole situation bewildered him. "Maybe." He rubbed his forehead. "Jessica and I were a great couple—one day everything was fine, the next she was hardly speaking to me. I've given this a lot of thought, trying to come up with some explanation for what happened. The only thing I can think of is that Elizabeth doesn't like me, and she talked Jessica into breaking up with me and then pressing charges."

The male professor studied James a moment before asking his question. "What makes you think Elizabeth doesn't like you?"

"I'm a Sigma, for one. She has a history of run-ins with the Sigma members. Also, she's probably worried about her sister meeting new guys, because Jessica's marriage didn't work out."

Jessica looked at James in disbelief. She was amazed at the intricate story he'd developed in his mind. He was rationalizing everything. Jessica's emotions were a mix of outrage and sadness. She could tell by his demeanor that he believed every word he was saying.

The male student who didn't say anything during Jessica's questioning spoke. "You're so calm. Aren't you mad that your car was wrecked, and that now you have to sit here and defend yourself?"

"It's not fun, but I know where Jessica is coming from," he said. "She's had a tough time with her marriage recently breaking up. I know she didn't want to mention this, but her ex-husband was shot and paralyzed by Jessica's brother. That's a lot for one person to deal with. I just hope that Jess can find another way to release her anger other than accusing people like me." There was a murmur from the crowd. James turned to Jessica, but she continued to look straight ahead. "Jessica," he said, speaking directly to her. "I'm sorry you think I hurt you. I just wanted to have a good time. That's all. I thought you wanted the same."

Jessica continued to look ahead, refusing to meet his gaze. Hot tears stung her eyes. She felt the eyes of the committee members on her, looking at her with pity. How did everything get so twisted? Jessica wanted to get up and run as fast as she could, away from everything. She didn't want to stay to hear the committee's decision—she knew what it was going to be. James was going to win.

"Please take me to the university," Lila told the cabdriver. Her throat ached as she tried to choke back the tears. *He's not coming,* she thought sadly. Her gaze was fixed on the main entrance of the hospital as the cab pulled away. *I should have known.*

The driver suddenly slammed on his brakes, and the cab screeched to a halt. "Hey, watch it!" he shouted out the window. A pedestrian had run in front of the car. "Watch where you're going!"

Suddenly the cab door flew open. Lila tried to see what was happening through her tears. She watched a blurry figure slide into the backseat.

"Sorry about that," he apologized to the cabdriver between gasps. "I was in a hurry." The cabdriver grumbled.

It sounded like Bruce. *Tell me I'm not dreaming,* Lila thought wistfully, unable to see clearly through her tears. She dried her eyes and looked again. It was true. Bruce was sitting right next to her, and he was holding an enormous box.

"These are for you." Bruce handed her the box. "I tied the bow myself," he added proudly.

Lila lifted the cover to find the most beautiful champagne roses she had ever seen. "Oh, Bruce, they're gorgeous!" Lila thought her heart would burst. "I thought you'd left. . . ." Her voice trailed off.

Bruce shook his head. "No—I mean, I did. I wanted to get you these, but I should've . . ." He stopped in mid-sentence. He was staring into her eyes so intensely, she felt as though she were melting.

Bruce put his arm around her shoulders and pressed her close to him. Lila became lost in the embrace. It was the feeling she'd longed for ever since the night they had been separated. She tilted her head back and closed her eyes in anticipation of his kiss.

Bruce's face was so close, Lila could almost feel his lips touch hers. But he hesitated. *Is he having second thoughts?* she wondered.

"What's wrong?" she asked, looking deeply into his eyes.

Bruce seemed transfixed, as though he were a

million miles away. Lila thought she felt his arms trembling.

"Nothing," Bruce answered, his voice filled with emotion. "It's just that—I love you, Lila."

Lila found herself unable to speak. Instead, she answered him with a passionate kiss.

The committee members filed back into the room. They seemed to move in slow motion, every minute dragging. Jessica was in agony. She just wanted the whole ordeal to be over.

Elizabeth squeezed Jessica's arm. During the committee's recess, Elizabeth had hardly said a word. Jessica knew that she was still reeling from James's accusations. "No matter what happens, we'll be here for you," she said as the committee members took their seats.

Dean Shreeve finally sat down. "Come to order." He waited for the room to quiet down. "As you all know, we're here because Ms. Wakefield has brought sexual assault charges against Mr. Montgomery."

Jessica swallowed hard. Time ground to a halt, and she felt as if she were suspended in the air, far away from her body, watching everything from a distance. All she could do was sit there and watch everything being played out before her.

"Ms. Wakefield, with regard to your charge—" Dean Shreeve paused and looked directly into her eyes. "This committee finds that you have not sufficiently proven your case."

Jessica felt herself being hurled back to reality with tremendous force. *It was all a waste of time.* Jessica thought of all the trouble she had been through and how difficult it had been to press charges. It had all been for nothing. She should never have come forward.

"Furthermore, it's the suggestion of the committee that you seek counseling. False accusations are very destructive, Ms. Wakefield. They can ruin people's lives."

Jessica hugged her sister to ease the sting of the dean's words.

He turned to James. "I thank you for your utmost patience and understanding, Mr. Montgomery. I'm sorry you had to endure this long process. You're free to leave."

"Thank you, sir," James answered. Several Sigmas clapped and cheered. Mariela and Alison were already at the front of the room, congratulating James.

"Take me home!" Jessica cried to Elizabeth. At any moment, she thought she would collapse. "I can't take any more. Please, just take me home."

Chapter Sixteen

When Elizabeth heard the verdict, she moved forward, ready to attack the committee, but Tom held her back. "Don't," he said, trying to calm her. "There's nothing you can do."

Elizabeth wrestled free from his grip and threw her arms around her sister. Jessica had been through so much—they had no right to humiliate her.

"I can't bear this," Jessica sobbed. Elizabeth saw that her sister's face was pale and she was shaking. She helped Jessica to her feet and turned around. Then she spotted the figure of a young woman in the doorway. It was Maia.

"Look," Elizabeth whispered to Jessica. They watched as Maia strode into the room and approached the committee. She spoke in a loud, clear voice. "Dean Shreeve, I would like a chance to speak before the committee," Maia said.

"It's too late. I'm afraid the committee has already made its decision, Ms.—"

"Stillwater. My name is Maia Stillwater," Maia said calmly. "I only ask for a moment of your time."

Before Dean Shreeve could protest, Maia approached the table and whispered to the dean. His eyes grew wide, then he said, "Very well, we will hear your testimony." He turned to James. "Mr. Montgomery, would you be so kind as to take your seat?"

James looked confused, his confidence slightly shaken. Mariela, who was hugging James, pulled away and went to the back of the room. The crowd watched silently, wondering what was going to happen next.

"Ms. Stillwater, you may proceed."

"Thank you," she said calmly. "I am here to support Jessica Wakefield's charge against James Montgomery."

Elizabeth stared at Maia in awe. She looked so different from the Maia she knew. The young woman standing in front of the committee was poised and cool, not fearful or timid. There was a lump in Elizabeth's throat. Maybe there was hope after all.

"Just like Jessica, I was also sexually assaulted by James . . . but unfortunately, no one came to my rescue. I was raped." Maia stood tall as she retold her story, and the committee members seemed entranced by what she had to say. Her voice was steady, never faltering. It was her moment to finally release all the pain and guilt she had been carrying with her, and Elizabeth thought that she was doing beautifully.

"I didn't tell anyone for a long time. I was too ashamed," Maia said. "I knew that because of James's reputation, no one would believe me. I finally broke down and told Elizabeth, and that's why she went after James and Jessica."

"I have a question," the male professor said. "Why are you coming forward now? Why did you wait so long?"

"I didn't press charges for the same reason I couldn't tell anyone—I was ashamed." Maia looked at Jessica. "But Jessica had the courage to come forward. I didn't want to testify at first, but I realized that she needed me. After I heard that James attacked her, I couldn't help but feel responsible—I thought that if only I had said something, it would have never happened. And I want to be sure it doesn't happen to anyone else. I also came for James." She turned to look at James, her gaze strong and steady. She spoke directly to him. "James, you have a problem and you need help. You can't continue to treat women this way. Sex isn't football—it's not a game."

Elizabeth's heart soared. She looked at Jessica, whose face was streaked with tears. *Everything is going to be fine,* she thought.

Just then, Elizabeth heard sobs coming from across the room. She looked up to see where the sound was coming from. Then she noticed James, his head buried in his hands.

Alex walked to the coffeehouse, feeling guilty. Here she was, about to go on her second date with Noah, and she was still thinking about T-Squared. *What am I doing?* Alex asked herself. *How can I go out with one guy and think about another?*

She saw Noah in the distance. *I have to tell him,* she thought. She wanted to start a relationship with Noah, but she couldn't if she didn't tell him the truth. It wouldn't be fair.

"Hi, Alex." Noah smiled.

"Hi," she answered. He looked so happy, she hated to ruin his mood.

"I'm glad you came," he said shyly. The soft light of the setting sun made his hair shine.

What if he doesn't want to see me anymore? Alex thought miserably. Noah was everything she wanted, and she was frightened at the thought of losing him. But keeping this from him would be wrong.

"It was nice of you to call me," she started. "But there's something I have to tell you."

Noah stared at her uneasily. "What is it?"

"I don't know how to say this." She paused. "I'm interested in someone else."

"Oh, my God, Maia—why didn't you tell me?" James cried, his shoulders shaking. Jessica watched as she brushed away her tears. It was satisfying for her to see him cry—to watch James experience pain the way she had.

"I did tell you," Maia said forcefully. "Over and over again I told you to stop. Why didn't you stop, James?"

James shook his head, as if he couldn't find an explanation. "I thought you were fooling around," he said weakly.

Despite Maia's cool exterior, there was a flash of anger in her eyes. "What did I have to do for you to take me seriously?"

"I don't know," he muttered through his tears. "I'm sorry for everything I've done." James's voice cracked. "I'm sorry, Jessica." The room was silent as James continued to cry, with his face buried in his hands. Jessica felt a pang of sadness for him—both his college career and his bright future were gone in one swift motion. The only thing that prevented Jessica from feeling pity was knowing he had brought it all upon himself.

The committee quietly conferred, and after a moment the dean spoke. "It's highly unusual for the committee to reconsider after a decision has been made, but then again, this is a highly unusual case. In light of Ms. Stillwater's testimony and Mr. Montgomery's confession, we have decided to reverse our decision. Mr. Montgomery is found guilty of the charge, his punishment to be determined at a separate hearing. Ms. Wakefield, please accept our deepest apologies."

The room was filled with an explosion of voices and movement. Jessica was instantly surrounded by Billie, Steven, Elizabeth, and all her friends. Fresh tears filled her eyes as they each hugged her in turn.

Jessica wept when she finally reached her sister. She hugged Elizabeth with all her strength. "I could never have done this without your help," Jessica whispered.

"I'm so proud of you," Elizabeth said to her twin.

Out of the corner of her eye, Jessica saw Maia standing nearby. "Thank you for coming, Maia. You were terrific," Jessica said as she turned to give her a hug. "You really came through for me."

Maia smiled wearily. "After I left your room this morning, I decided that I couldn't let you do it all alone." She started to tremble. "I don't know how I ever got the courage to testify."

"It's finally over." Elizabeth sighed, hugging them both. "Now we can forget about it."

"I don't know if we'll ever be able to forget about it," Maia said solemnly, "but at least we can move on."

"What?" Noah was in shock. Did he hear her correctly?

"I'm interested in someone else," Alex repeated.

Noah was crushed. He sat down on the bench, unable to comprehend what he had just heard. It was Todd Wilkins. He should have known. After everything he had been through to get together with

Alex, he was going to lose her to Todd.

"Who is he?" Noah finally managed to ask. He had to hear the answer from her lips.

Alex paused. "It's going to sound ridiculous, but it's someone I've never met. When I was having some personal problems, I called this campus hot line and spoke with this guy. Ever since, I haven't been able to get him out of my mind." She looked at him. "Are you all right?"

Noah looked at her and smiled. "You wouldn't be talking about someone named T-Squared, would you?"

"How did you know?" She looked at him in confusion.

Noah was so happy, he thought his heart would burst. "Enid—it's me," he said.

Alex's eyes were wide, and Noah watched with delight as the news sank in. "You're T-Squared?" she said incredulously. "How long have you known—"

"I just figured it out the last time you called," he said.

They stared at each other for a long moment, then broke out into laughter.

"I can't believe it," she said after she caught her breath. "It's really you. And all this time I thought I was interested in two different guys."

Noah relaxed. Suddenly, they didn't have the pressure of trying to get to know each other. They'd been getting acquainted for the last few weeks. "After all those phone calls, I feel like we've been dating for a long time."

Alex smiled. She leaned over and gave him a soft kiss on the lips. "That's for helping me through everything," she said. "I've been wanting to do that for a long time."

Noah smiled. "You've been wanting to kiss Noah or T-Squared?"

Alex thought about it. "I've been wanting to kiss *you*."

Noah touched her cheek. "Your wait is over," he said as he returned her kiss.

Chapter
Seventeen

"What are you doing here?" William hissed through clenched teeth. "I told you never to meet me here."

"I couldn't help it, William. I missed you." Celine started taking books off the cart and randomly placing them on the library shelves.

"Give me that!" William yanked a book out of her hand. Students at a nearby table looked up to see what all the commotion was about. William wheeled himself backward into the stacks with one hand, dragging Celine by the elbow with the other.

"Ow!" she said loudly, nearly tripping over the wheels. "What's wrong with you?"

He looked around to see if anyone was watching. "Don't you know how dangerous it is for us to be seen together? Someone might figure things out." His ice-blue eyes flared in anger. "What do you want?"

Celine pouted, girlishly twirling a curl around her

finger. "I haven't seen you in a while. You said we were going to have dinner together."

William continued replacing the books on the shelves, not looking at Celine as he spoke. "I've had trouble sneaking out at night. Andrea's been out sick."

Celine stood behind him and wrapped her arms around his neck. Who did Willie think he was fooling, anyway? She knew he had been sneaking around, hot on the princess's trail. "Come on, William," she said out loud. "I know you've been keeping tabs on her."

William's face turned bright red. He looked as though he were going to explode. "Keep your voice down!"

"Careful, Willie! We wouldn't want you to blow a gasket." She flashed him her best debutante smile.

"Did you deliver the note?" he snapped.

"I put it right where it belongs," she answered innocently. *Right in the trash can.*

"Good. I have another one for you."

"Shame on you!" She waved a perfectly manicured fingernail in front of his face. "How can you ask me to do you a favor when you treat me so badly?"

William gripped his head between his hands. Celine had seen that look of frustration only once before, and it was dangerous. If they hadn't been in a public place, she would have started running. "I'm sorry," he said, trying to keep his anger under control. "Maybe we could have dinner together later this week."

"That's so sweet of you, hon. But my calendar's all booked up. Let's try next month."

"Celine . . ." William's voice was taking an ominous tone. "I need you to deliver that note for me. I'm not asking you—I'm telling you."

She ignored him. "Well, look who's coming," Celine said, peering through the stacks. Elizabeth had just walked through the front door and was heading in their direction. "Looks like you can just hand it to her yourself."

"Hey, man, it's good to see you!" Tony Calvieri said as he shook Bruce's hand. The other Sigmas gathered around to welcome back their president.

"It's good to be here," Bruce said, loving the attention. "I hope you guys upheld the Sigma reputation while I was gone."

"Of course we did!" Jeff Cross shouted. "Party every night!" Bruce laughed. He lounged on the plaid couch, taking it all in. Everything was just as he remembered. It really was good to be back. "So, fill me in on the latest Sigma news."

"You know that James is out, right?" said Andy Hoffer.

"Out of the house?" Bruce asked.

"No, out of school. He was kicked out."

Bruce stared at Peter Wilbourne, who was nodding to confirm the story. "And you know whose fault it is? That wench, Jessica Wakefield's."

Bruce shook his head, trying to comprehend what they were saying. Apparently more had gone on while he was away than he originally thought. "Would someone explain this to me?"

Bill Montana cut in. "You know that James was dating Jessica, right? Well, things started heating up between the two of them, and she couldn't handle it. So she blew the whistle on him. She started telling everyone that he tried to rape her. And guess what? The school believed her."

Peter pounded his fist into his open palm. "Wait till I get my hands on that little liar. I'm going to make her life hell."

"Just chill out a minute." Bruce tried to make sense of it all. Could James really do something like that? He'd heard James got pretty out of control when he was drunk. It wasn't unthinkable. And sure, Jessica could twist things to get her way when she wanted to—but not with something this big. She wasn't a liar.

"Look," Bruce said. "Wakefield may be a lot of things, but a liar isn't one of them."

"Don't tell me you're siding with her." Peter stared at Bruce, anger flashing in his eyes.

"I'm not siding with anyone—I'm just telling you what I know." Bruce met Peter's stare. "I'm sorry James was kicked out, but there's nothing we can do."

"Oh yes, there is." Peter grinned evilly.

Bruce refused to back down. "If you so much as lay a hand on Jessica, you're out of here so fast your head will spin. That goes for all of you," he said, looking around the room. "If I hear that any of you have given Jessica a hard time—you're out of this fraternity."

Peter stormed out of the room in defeat. The rest of the Sigmas stared at Bruce with a combination of disbelief and awe.

"Is that clear to everyone?" Bruce asked. They nodded. "Good. Today is a big day for me, and I don't want you bozos to ruin it."

Tony laughed. "What's up?"

Bruce lay back on the couch and put his hands behind his head. "Today I go to pick up my new Jeep."

"What?" Jeff said with mock surprise. "You're not going to buy a new plane?"

"Very funny," Bruce said. "I've decided to stay on the ground for a while. This is a special-order, limited-edition Jeep Cherokee in fire-engine red."

Tony whistled. "With a machine like that, you're going to have women beating down your door."

"It doesn't matter," Bruce said. "There's only one woman I care about, and it would take a lot more than a Jeep to impress her."

"I just hope you're better at handling the Jeep than you are at flying a plane," Bill teased. "Or you're going to spend a lot of time driving around town by yourself."

*　　*　　*

217

Elizabeth scanned the main floor of the library, looking for the guy in the wheelchair. She had been so wrapped up in the hearing, she'd nearly forgotten to return the sonnet book.

She gripped the book in her hand. She hoped she would be able to just hand over the book, quickly thank him, then be on her way. The last thing she wanted was to be stuck talking to him while his eyes wandered all over her body. She shivered just thinking about it.

Elizabeth heard laughter coming from the reference section. It was a high-pitched, shrieking kind of laugh meant to draw attention. It was a laugh that she had heard many times before, and it always sent shivers down her spine. What was Celine doing here? In the few agonizing months that they had been roommates, Celine had never looked at a book, much less gone to the library. She probably didn't even know they had one on campus.

"Elizabeth!" Celine shouted when she saw her. Everyone seemed to be staring in their direction. Elizabeth wanted to crawl under a desk out of embarrassment.

"Celine," Elizabeth whispered, hoping she would get the hint. "How are you?"

"Oh, it's just so good to see you!" Celine squeezed her tightly.

Elizabeth thought she was going to suffocate from the strong scent of her perfume. *What's gotten into her?* Elizabeth wondered. Celine usually looked at her as though she wanted to claw her eyes out.

"Same here," Elizabeth answered stiffly. "So what are you doing in the library?"

"I'm working on a paper," Celine said awkwardly.

Elizabeth tried not to laugh. The only thing Celine ever studied was her fingernails. "What's the paper about?"

"You know, stuff." Celine seemed to have immediately lost interest in the conversation.

"I have to go," Elizabeth said, looking for an excuse to duck out. "I have to return this book."

"He's over there," Celine said, pointing to the stacks.

Elizabeth looked down the aisle. The man in the wheelchair was there.

How did she know I was looking for him? Elizabeth wondered as she walked over to where he was. She didn't remember mentioning it in the conversation. Well, if there was anything she could count on, it was the fact that Celine would keep getting stranger and stranger. Elizabeth's spine tingled as she approached the library assistant.

"Here's your book. Thanks." Elizabeth unceremoniously handed him the book.

He stared at her. "Did you like it?" he asked.

"It was great," Elizabeth responded abruptly. She turned to leave. "Thanks again. The book was a lifesaver," she said over her shoulder.

"I'm glad to hear it, Elizabeth," he answered softly.

*　　　*　　　*

Lila was lying on her bed, dreamily staring at the ceiling. It had been strange sleeping indoors for the past several days; she had grown used to the wide-open spaces and the warmth of Bruce's arms around her. Even though she was miserable out in the cold, Lila had loved staring up at the sky at night. In the dark of the Sierra Nevada, the stars sparkled more brilliantly than all the diamonds on Rodeo Drive. Lila had tried to count them every night, until she fell asleep.

"Put one right over there," Lila said to Jessica as she pointed to a blank spot on the ceiling.

"Where?" Jessica tried to steady herself on the stepladder.

"See the moon in the corner, and the shooting star over there? Put it right in between the two."

Jessica pulled the paper off the back of the glow-in-the-dark sticker and stuck it in the correct spot. "There. Are we done now?"

Lila studied the ceiling with a critical eye. "Not quite. I think there's one more package."

Jessica sighed. "Don't you think you have enough already? We've used nine packages. This place is going to be so bright, you won't be able to sleep."

Lila rolled her eyes. "You don't understand; it has to be just like it was in the mountains. It has to be perfect." She fluffed up her pillow. "Don't bunch them up too much," she said, critiquing Jessica's replica of the Big Dipper.

220

Jessica, whose back was beginning to ache, started sticking the stars on the ceiling at random. "You're the only person I've ever heard of who, after surviving a near-death experience in the wilderness, tries to re-create it."

Lila stuck out her tongue playfully. She was suddenly startled by the sound of a beeping car horn outside her window. Without looking, Lila headed out the door. "That must be Bruce!" she shouted. She stopped and looked at Jessica. "See you later—and do a good job!"

"Hey—where are you going?" Jessica asked, but she was too late. Lila was gone.

Lila stepped out into the bright sunlight. Parked behind her building was a brand-new, fire-engine-red Jeep Grand Cherokee, Ltd. There was a surfboard strapped to the roof.

Bruce smiled at her from behind the wheel. "Do you like it?"

"It's a beauty," Lila said.

"I was just on my way to the beach. Do you want to come?" Bruce smiled.

"Maybe," Lila said coyly. Ever since they'd returned to school, she and Bruce had been so busy that they hadn't had a moment alone together. "Although you don't have a very good record for being prepared when you go on trips," she teased.

Bruce frowned. "But I am this time."

Lila eyed him skeptically. "Do you have a full tank of gas?"

Bruce looked at the gauge. "Yep."

"How about food?" Lila asked.

He held up a cooler.

"Blanket?"

"In the back," Bruce said.

Lila thought for a minute. "Spare tire, first-aid kit, map?"

"Check, check, check."

"Hair curlers?"

"Hair curlers?" Bruce looked confused.

"You never know when they might come in handy. . . ."

Bruce shrugged, then smiled. "Check."

"How do I know I can trust you? How do I know you're not lying to me?" Lila said as she opened the passenger-side door.

"You don't," Bruce teased as he started the engine. "You're just going to have to find out for yourself."

Lila laughed. "Before I foolishly put my life in your hands again, I need you to stop at Theta House so I can pick up a few things I left there."

"Anything you say," Bruce said as he threw the Jeep into gear.

When they reached Theta House, Lila told Bruce to drive around to the back. "I'll just slip in the back door, grab my stuff, and we'll be off," she said.

"You mean I'll finally have you all to myself?" Bruce said as he swung around to the back of the house. "I can't believe it."

Chapter Eighteen

Bruce and Lila stared at the large group of Thetas and Sigmas that had congregated on the lawn behind the house. Paper lanterns hung from the back porch. Barbecues were set up, and tropical music was blaring from stereo speakers someone had put in front of an open window. A banner painted in bright colors was suspended between two trees. It read "Aloha, Bruce and Lila."

"SURPRISE!" the crowd screamed when they spotted the Jeep. Bruce and Lila looked at each other. "It's for us—I guess we'd better go," Lila said, a hint of disappointment in her voice.

"That's OK." Bruce gave her a quick kiss on the lips. "Maybe we can sneak out early."

They climbed out of the Jeep. "A luau for us?" Lila shouted happily. "Who would have believed it?"

Bruce stood there, dumbfounded, trying to match Lila's level of enthusiasm. He really had to hand it to her—Lila knew how to handle any social situation with grace and poise. "This is great!" he said.

Magda gave them each a plastic lei and a kiss on the cheek. "It's great to have you both back," she said.

Each of the Thetas and the Sigmas came up to them in turn, giving them hugs or shaking hands. Bruce had never doubted that their absence would have an effect on the campus. But at this moment, seeing so many faces that were happy to see both of them, Bruce realized for the first time just how nice it was to be missed.

Jeff Cross handed Bruce a pineapple shell filled with punch. Then he stood back, pounded his fists on his chest like Tarzan, and shouted "PARTY!" at the top of his lungs. Someone turned up the music.

The crowd parted in the middle, and making their way through were Isabella and her boyfriend, Danny. They stood several feet apart, each holding up an end of a long broom handle. "It's limbo time!" someone shouted, and the crowd responded instantly, forming a huge line behind the broom handle. One by one they bent themselves backward under the bar, swaying in time to the music.

Bruce spotted Lila surrounded by a group of Thetas, who were helping her put a grass skirt on over her shorts. "Is there something I can do to help?" Bruce asked.

Lila hit him playfully. "Would you like to try one on?"

"No, thanks." Bruce waved his hands and backed away.

"I think you'd look cute in a grass skirt," Denise said, sifting through the pile. She held one up. "And I think this one right here is just about your size."

Before he had a chance to run and hide, a few of the Thetas grabbed Bruce's arms and pulled him back.

"What's the matter, Patman?" Lila said, putting an orchid in her hair. "You're not secure enough in your manhood to play a little joke?"

"It's not that . . ."

Lila was already fastening the skirt around his waist. A pink orchid was tucked behind his left ear.

"Beautiful," Denise said.

Isabella nodded. "A work of art."

"Hmmm," Lila said. "I think he needs a little eyeliner."

Before any more damage could be done, Bruce firmly grabbed Lila by the hand. "Come on," he said. "Let's limbo."

"Can I interest you in a pineapple hot dog or a papaya burger?" Winston Egbert said to Jessica.

"No, thanks," Jessica answered dryly as she stared at the strange meat cooking on the grill. "I'm going to stick to the fruit."

"You don't know what you're missing." Winston flipped a burger. A gust of wind came up and blew the smoke in his face. Winston had a coughing fit.

"Are you all right?" Jessica asked. She handed

him some punch and waved the smoke away.

"Thanks," Winston wheezed between coughs.

"Where's Denise?" Jessica said, twirling a miniature umbrella with her fingers.

Winston took off his chef's hat. "She's over on the porch, trying to teach those girls how to do the hula." He pointed in her direction. Denise was in a grass skirt, gracefully moving her hips and moving her arms gently like waves on the ocean. "She's so beautiful," Winston said wistfully.

Jessica smiled. The next-best thing to being in love was to see someone else in love. "Why don't you join her?" Jessica asked.

"I can't," Winston said, wiping his sweaty forehead with his arm. "I have pineapple hot dog duty. They'll burn if I leave."

Jessica tried not to laugh as she glanced over at the black, shriveled pieces of meat on the barbecue. "Actually, Win, I think they'll burn even if you're here." She gave him a pat on the back, then snatched the tongs out of his hand. "I'll take over for you. Go and have a good time with your hula girl."

"Thanks, Jess," Winston said gratefully. He took off his apron and handed it to her. "Just remember that the papaya burgers have to be well cooked on both sides." He started to walk away. "Oh, yeah. In about an hour, they're going to bring out kiwi kebobs, so make sure you leave room on the grill for those!"

"Don't worry, I will!" Jessica waited until

Winston had completely turned around before dumping the burnt hot dogs and burgers in the trash.

Jessica felt someone standing beside her. She looked up. It was Mariela. "Can I talk to you?" she asked.

"Sure," Jessica answered. *Is she going to yell at me?* she wondered as she continued to scrape the grill.

"I'm sorry I didn't believe you," Mariela said apologetically. "You were just trying to help me, and I turned against you. I'm sorry."

Jessica put a hand on her sorority sister's shoulder. "It's all right—I understand. I can see why it would be hard to believe. I didn't even want to believe it myself."

Mariela wiped away a tear that rolled down her cheek. "I feel so stupid," she said, trying to regain her composure. "I'm so mad at myself for falling for it." She looked at Jessica. "When I think that I could've been next—I get so scared."

Jessica reached over and gave her a hug. "Don't think about it. Everything turned out fine."

Mariela returned the hug. "Can you forgive me?" she asked.

Jessica pulled away. "It's over, Mariela. Let's forget about it."

"OK." Mariela smiled.

Alex walked over to Jessica, carrying a huge platter. "Are you the chef?"

Jessica was startled. "Alex! You look great," she said as she put on the chef's hat.

Alex grinned. "Thanks. I feel great too."

Mariela pointed to Noah, who was playing volleyball. "Who's that hunky guy you're here with?" she asked.

"That's Noah," Alex said shyly. "We just started going out."

"Nice work!" Jessica said as she took the platter from Alex. "Are these the kiwi kebobs?" she asked.

"I guess so—Magda told me to bring them to the chef." Alex started to walk back to the house. "There's more in the kitchen. I'll go get them."

Jessica stared at the huge pile of green skewers. She looked at Mariela. "Do you know anything about cooking kiwi kebobs?" Jessica asked.

Mariela laughed, wiping away her tears. "No, but I could try."

Jessica handed her a set of tongs. "Here—you load them onto the grill, and I'll round up some poor suckers to eat them."

Elizabeth opened the door to the library stacks and walked in. It was completely dark. She turned on the lights. No one was there.

She scanned the stacks for a book of sonnets. It should have been easy to find, but all the books were in the wrong order. It looked like someone had dumped them on the shelves without even looking. There were stacks and stacks of books, piled high on tables and chairs, on the floor. Books started dropping from the ceiling, adding to the piles. Elizabeth started to cry. She'd have to go through the piles, one at a time, if she wanted to find the book.

Suddenly she heard a noise coming from the back of the room. She saw a glimmer of metal, then wheels rolling out from behind the bookshelves. It was a wheelchair.

"Get away from me!" Elizabeth screamed at the bearded man in the chair. She threw a pile of books in his way, but he stood up and started walking toward her.

She tried to run, but books were falling all around her. She covered her head. A huge volume of Shakespeare's works fell at her feet and she tripped, crashing to the floor.

The man loomed closer, his ice-blue eyes sparkling. Elizabeth tried to move, but she was trapped. When he was right over her, she reached up and ripped off his beard. It was William White.

Elizabeth sat up in bed, bathed in sweat. Her heart was pounding in her chest, and it was hard for her to breathe. She looked over at Jessica, who was sleeping soundly in her bed.

This is crazy, Elizabeth thought. *William is locked up. Why am I still dreaming about him?*

Elizabeth got out of bed and switched on a night-light. She had been so frightened by the dream that it would take hours to get back to sleep. She paced the room to try to calm herself down. As she glanced around the room nervously, she caught sight of a note under the door.

Elizabeth swallowed hard. She reached down and grabbed the slip of paper. She held it in her shaking hand for several minutes, then she finally opened it.

Make but my name thy love, and that love still,
And then thou lovest me, for my name is Will.

The note slipped out of Elizabeth's hand and dropped to the floor. She covered her mouth to stifle her screams.

Elizabeth doesn't know that her most dangerous enemy is on the loose—and out to get her. Find out what happens when Elizabeth and William White meet face-to-face in Sweet Valley University Thriller Edition #2, HE'S WATCHING YOU.

SIGN UP FOR THE
SWEET VALLEY HIGH®
FAN CLUB!

Hey, girls! Get all the gossip on Sweet
Valley High's® most popular teenagers
when you join our fantastic Fan Club!
As a member, you'll get all of this really
cool stuff:

- Membership Card with your own
  personal Fan Club ID number
- A Sweet Valley High® Secret
  Treasure Box
- Sweet Valley High® Stationery
- Official Fan Club Pencil (for secret
  note writing!)
- Three Bookmarks
- A "Members Only" Door Hanger
- Two Skeins of J. & P. Coats® Embroidery
  Floss with flower barrette instruction
  leaflet
- Two editions of *The Oracle* newsletter
- Plus exclusive Sweet Valley High®
  product offers, special savings,
  contests, and much more!

Be the first to find out what Jessica & Elizabeth Wakefield are up to by joining the
Sweet Valley High® Fan Club for the one-year membership fee of only $6.25 each
for U.S. residents, $8.25 for Canadian residents (U.S. currency). Includes shipping
& handling.

Send a check or money order (do not send cash) made payable to "Sweet Valley
High® Fan Club" along with this form to:

SWEET VALLEY HIGH® FAN CLUB, BOX 3919-B, SCHAUMBURG, IL 60168-3919

NAME_____
(Please print clearly)

ADDRESS_____

CITY_____ STATE _____ ZIP_____
(Required)

AGE _____ BIRTHDAY_____ /_____ /_____

It's Your First Love. . . Yours *and* His.

Love Stories

Nobody Forgets Their First Love!

Now there's a romance series that gets to the heart of *everyone's* feelings about falling in love. *Love Stories* reveals how boys feel about being in love, too! In every story, a boy and girl experience the real-life ups and downs of being a couple, and share in the thrills, joys, and sorrows of first love.

MY FIRST LOVE, Love Stories #1
0-553-56661-X $3.50/$4.50 Can.

SHARING SAM, Love Stories #2
0-553-56660-1 $3.50/$4.50 Can.

Bantam Doubleday Dell
Books For Young Readers   BFYR 104-7/94